An Outback AFFAIR

IRIS LEACH

Author of *Looking for Prince Charming*
and *A Taste of Honey*

CRIMSON
ROMANCE
F+W Media, Inc.

This edition published by
Crimson Romance
an imprint of F+W Media, Inc.
10151 Carver Road, Suite 200
Blue Ash, Ohio 45242
www.crimsonromance.com

ISBN 10: 1-4405-6439-6
ISBN 13: 978-1-4405-6439-0
eISBN 10: 1-4405-6440-X
eISBN 13: 978-1-4405-6440-6

For Cheryl

My very special girl.

AI

PROLOGUE

The shock of seeing her name displayed in the shop window brought Joel Caine to an abrupt stop. *Photographic studies by C. Trenhaile.* Squinting, he read the shop sign—Paradox Photos. No way, couldn't be her, and with a nonchalant shrug, he continued on his way down the street. But her name repeated in his brain like a mantra...Ms C. Trenhaile. Could the C stand for Claudia— Claudia Trenhaile?

What if it is her?

Nah, couldn't be.

But what if it is?

A coincidence, but then he didn't believe in coincidences. Two women sporting the name Claudia Trenhaile, and both of them crossing his path was too much of a coincidence. So, logically thinking, it was her.

There had never been closure. Not for his brother, their mother, or for him either. At the time they had been too grief-stricken over Luke's death to follow through and call on Claudia Trenhaile. The years passed and then it was too late.

Drop it, Caine, let sleeping dogs lie. Let it ride, and all the other clichés that really said, coward, face the past, kill it off, and give it a decent burial.

Damn. He backtracked and studied the photograph of the young boy. The blond curls, the dark blue eyes, the stubborn tilt of his chin. He jerked back; his heart slammed against his chest wall. My God, it couldn't be. Could it? This boy was the image of his brother, Luke.

Bending forward, he pressed his face close to the glass. A tall woman was working at the rear of the shop, but he couldn't make out her features or her hair color.

Forget it and keep on walking.

What the hell, I have to know.

Joel straightened and set his mouth in what he hoped was an I'm-not-afraid-to-face-the-past line, rolled his shoulders, and walked into the shop.

CHAPTER ONE

Cassie Trenhaile glanced over at the window. In the park across the road from her apartment, the sulphur-crested cockatoos fed on the grass seeds. The beauty of the wattle trees paraded their sun-bright yellow blossoms under the clear blue sky with its broad glow of soft, mellow sunshine. Yet this was Melbourne, and the beautiful day could quickly turn into icy cold winds or wild storms and rain.

Noises of a child playing brought her mind back to the moment. "Sam, are you getting dressed or are you playing?"

The noise stopped. She heard the soft shuffle of bare feet. "I'm getting dressed."

She gave a tiny laugh. "Good boy. Breakfast is ready."

"I'm coming, Aunty C."

She smiled as he entered the kitchen. Maybe she viewed him through rose-colored glasses, but to her he was a most beautiful child, and not only in his looks but in his gentle and giving nature. In all of their time together, she'd received only love and happiness, and she thanked God for him. Her heart melted with love.

He gave a perplexed look. "I can't find my sneakers."

Her gaze travelled to his feet. "You're wearing two different socks."

He pouted his bottom lip and stared rather objectively at his feet, his toes curling up to meet his gaze. He looked up at her, his blue eyes wide and innocent. "They're both blue," he concluded.

Laughing softly, she swept him into her arms and kissed his rosy cheek. Oh, how she loved the feel of him, the smell of him.

He was her very life's reason. He wrapped his arms around her neck and squeezed as hard as he could. She kissed him again, and lowered him to the floor. "Did you look under the bed for your sneakers?"

"Yep."

"Yes, Sam, not yep," she corrected automatically. "Did you look under the dresser?"

"Yep, I mean yes."

"Couch?" His eyes brightened and he scampered into the lounge-room, returning with his sneakers held above his head like a gold cup after winning a race. "Well done, Sam."

Cassie poured cold milk over his cereal and sprinkled the top with slices of banana. She placed the bowl in front of him, as well as a small koala-shaped tumbler with orange juice. He took a thirsty swallow and wiped his mouth with the back of his arm. "Hey, why use your hand when you've got a sleeve?" Cassie scolded gently.

He giggled, picked up a napkin, and wiped his mouth, waiting for her approval. "Good boy," she said, not disappointing him.

Cassie placed the dirty dishes into hot, soapy water and her mind roved back to the day Claudia had sobbed that she was pregnant, that she hadn't known until it was too late for a medical abortion, that she had spotting and linked it with an unusual menstrual cycle. Cassie had breathed a sigh of relief. Although deeply believing that every woman had the right to choose, abortion would never have been her own choice.

The toast popped and Cassie buttered and spread raspberry jam over the crispy slices. She placed the plate in front of Sam and turned back to the sink.

Claudia had told her the name of the father, saying he didn't love her and that he'd broken off their relationship months ago when she'd learned the awful truth—he was married and refused to leave his wife. Claudia became hysterical when Cassie had said he had a right to know about the baby, until eventually she'd agreed that he'd lost his rights when he had lied and cheated two innocent women.

Six weeks after Sam had been born Claudia was killed in an automobile accident.

"I've finished, Aunty."

She spun around. "Want more toast?"

He shook his head and, placing his hand under his chin, said, "I'm full up to here."

"That's pretty full," she said, shepherding Sam into the bathroom and watching over him as he cleaned his teeth.

She knelt down and kissed the tip of his nose. "Do you know how much I love you?"

"Yep." He held his arms outstretched. "This much."

"Just checking."

"And I'll love you more when my arms get bigger. Won't I, Aunty C?"

"Sure thing, Sam." She took him by the hand. "Okay, let's go to the park."

CHAPTER TWO

Cassie curled up on the sofa to read a mystery novel she'd started the night before.

At the sound of her doorbell, she glanced up, tossed her book aside, and walked to the front door.

A man filled her doorway. "Yes?" She ran her eyes up and down his muscular body—tall and good-looking with his blond cowlick and blue-eyed stare and sexier than any man had a right to be. "May I help you?"

"I'm looking for Claudia Trenhaile."

Pain speared Cassie's heart. After all these years it still hurt. "I'm afraid Claudia died over three years ago."

He blanched. "I didn't know—didn't realize." He stared down at her. "And you are?"

"Her sister, Cassie." This man was making her nervous. Why?

He held out a hand. "The name's Joel Caine. Does that ring a bell?"

Joel Caine! Dear God, he was Sam's uncle. Of all the people in the world, he was the last person she'd expected to knock on her door. What did he want? Why had he sought out Claudia after all these years?

She made to close the door, but he prevented her by placing his hands on the wood frame. "We need to talk."

His face was bleak, and she experienced a tiny flash of empathy. *I can handle this.*

But Joel Caine? The brother of the man who had destroyed her sister's life.

Pull yourself together.

She didn't want any part of this—whatever this may be, and she knew she wasn't handling the situation well. She resisted the impulse to slam the door in his face.

Her eyes filled with tears, but she gained composure quickly and said, "Why are you here, Mr. Caine? Why you and not your brother?"

"Luke—my brother died." His voice broke. "A plane crash."

Shock rattled through her. "I'm sorry. It seems they were a star-crossed couple, your brother and my sister."

"Fate wasn't kind to them, that's for sure."

Emotions twisted and split. She looked at him, knowing if he'd knocked on her door selling vacuum cleaners, she'd have trusted him. Would have found those eyes of his frank and honest—compelling. "I can't understand why you'd come to my home, Mr. Caine. What you want from me."

"I had business in Melbourne. I passed an art studio displaying some of your work. Trenhaile is such an unusual name that it immediately caught my attention."

"And—?"

"And I asked the owner about you—I mean, Claudia. I assumed the C stood for Claudia. They assumed I was interested in hiring your photographic services so they gave me your business card with your address."

"I see. Well, I'm sorry you've had a wasted trip." She made to close the door, and again his big hand prevented her.

"May I come in for a moment?"

She hesitated, knowing this wasn't just a friendly visit. That Joel Caine had a more dire reason for his visit. "Of course."

He moved quickly inside the room. Cassie followed him into the lounge room.

"It's complicated and extremely difficult for me." He smiled without amusement.

"I don't understand, Mr. Caine."

She studied his imposing figure sensing a masculine strength, an unwitting natural dominance about him that other men lacked. It showed in his physical power, the flash of his perceptive blue eyes and the set of his mouth. Big and strong, his size alone gave a picture of command simmering just below the surface. He was undeniably sensual. Another time, another place, and she'd like to take her interest in him further.

He shrugged, turned his head to one side as if something had suddenly caught his interest, then back to connect with her. "In the window of the shop there was a study of a small boy."

Her world tilted and nausea burned her throat as if she'd swallowed acid. *He knows about Sam.* She was unsure what to do now. How to handle this situation.

"I asked the owner and she said he's your son," he said quietly, firmly, as if daring her to deny that Sam existed. "Is he your son, Miss Trenhaile?"

Her skin heated. She had such an overwhelming response to the man, her mouth went dry, her heart raced, and she was afraid. Joel Caine could turn her world upside-down. Threaten the very existence she'd worked so hard to obtain. The life she'd made with Sam—the contentment in knowing she could support them and give him all that he needed. "He's my nephew."

His head jerked, face pale. "He is Luke's son. The resemblance...I knew instinctively."

She drew in a sharp breath, her fingers playing nervously with the collar of her shirt. "Yes, he's Luke's son."

He lowered his eyes. "We need to talk."

"Talk?" She searched his face looking for God knows what— sympathy, empathy, regret maybe. "What could we possibly talk about?" Her head tugged back. "Hmm, maybe the way your brother treated my sister shamelessly, do you think?" Her voice held not a trace of sarcasm or accusation—just the facts, ma'am.

"The way he dumped her pregnant and alone. Is this what you want to talk about, Mr. Caine?"

Surprise registered on his face. "I'm sure he didn't know about the baby." His voice was shaky, croaky.

She tapped her forehead with the heel of her hand. "Of course he didn't, stupid me. He'd long gone."

"Bad things happen," he said gently. "It's part and parcel of life." His forehead furrowed and his blue eyes flashed.

She was shocked at his abrupt dismissal of the sordid affair between Claudia and Luke. "You don't seem to think your brother has done anything wrong." She drew a ragged breath through her nostrils. "That it doesn't matter that he lied and cheated on his wife and a girl who thought he loved her."

Joel reached out and she drew back from him. "I know this must be difficult for you."

Trepidation pirouetted around her brain. Why was she so wary of this man?

I don't want him here in my home. He scares me.

Hear him out and get rid of him.

He wants something.

A presentiment, strong, scary, and totally real filled her chest.

She took another step backwards. He moved a little closer, and a whiff of his spicy cologne circled her. With a shaky hand, she brushed back a fallen lock of her hair. "It's not that it's difficult. You've come at a bad time."

He glanced casually around. "Entertaining?"

She bristled. Arrogant twerp. "I'm unprepared for visitors."

He refrained from answering. What could he say, her answer so inane.

"I'd like to see my nephew."

Was the emphasis on the word "my," as if somehow she had deliberately deceived him? Kept Sam hidden from him? "That's not possible."

"Why?"

"Sam's asleep."

"I'd simply look at him."

"I don't want him disturbed."

He grinned, her heart constricted, her head swirled. She closed her eyes.

"I'd put a church mouse to shame."

She shrugged her consent and showed him into Sam's bedroom. Leaning against the doorjamb, she watched him approach Sam's bed.

He didn't move for such a long time as he stared down at the sleeping child. Her heart practiced back flips as his big hand lowered and gently touched the shining curls of his nephew's head.

They remained silent until they were back in the lounge room. His voice was husky when he said, "He's a fine looking boy."

"Yes, he is."

He glanced cursively around the room. "May I sit?"

"Of course."

He spread out on the opposite end of the sofa to where she was standing, dangling one long arm over the arm of the sofa, the other slung carelessly along the top. She turned her face away from him. He was so relaxed while she was as tight as a miser's purse. Feeling him watching her, she turned and locked eyes with him.

"We have a lot to talk about."

"So you keep telling me." She shrugged. "You have something in mind, Mr. Caine? And of course it's to do with Sam."

"Yes, it's to do with Sam."

She was unable to hold back her question. "What is it you want?"

"Sam to come home with me."

Cassie's world titled on its axis.

Bile rose in her throat. Was the man insane? "Come home with you?" she repeated, trying to make sense of the words.

A small tight smile. "I want to get to know him and him me."
She rubbed her upper arms absently as though she were cold.
The chill wasn't in the air; it was in her heart. "You can't have him."
For a long moment he remained silent, just stared at her. "You
can't deny me access to Sam."

She struggled to keep her voice normal. "Yes, yes I can. I have
full custody of him." That wasn't altogether true, as she'd never
bothered to obtain legal custody. At the time it hadn't seemed
important; there was no one else interested in his welfare.

He briefly closed his eyes, pressing his fingers against closed
lids. "I never knew about him until now," he reasoned. "If I had
known—"

"You would have done what, Mr. Caine?" She swallowed down
the lump in her throat; her fear now a reckless panic threatening
to overtake her common sense. "Fought me in court for him?
Whisked him away to foreign places?"

"I had every right to know about him," he muttered. His blue
eyes darkened. "It's you who made the mistake, Miss Trenhaile,
when you decided to keep Sam from his paternal family."

His response confused her and she struggled for an answer.
"I've raised him since he was six weeks old," she said quietly, not
so her heart, which was hammering against her ribs.

"I realize that." He sighed. "But I'm his uncle, and we have a
right to know each other. I have the right to be in his life as much
as you." His eyes flared blue ice. "I won't be denied him. Know
this and accept it."

"Are you threatening me, Mr. Caine?"

"Just stating facts, Miss Trenhaile." He studied her face. "There
are other aspects to consider."

"Such as?"

"Sam is my heir."

She wet her lips. "What?" A knot formed in her throat. "What
did you say?"

"He'll eventually inherit everything I own." His eyes narrowed as if waiting for a reaction.

He wasn't to be disappointed as shock rushed through her and she gasped. "You're wealthy?"

"I own property. Good property and I've been doing really well the last couple of years, despite the drought."

The silence became unnerving. He stood, moving closer to her, and she instinctively took a step backwards. He rubbed his fingers across the stubble of his chin. "We can do this the easy way or the hard way."

"The easy way?"

"You do as I ask."

"The hard way?"

"I'll convince you."

She didn't doubt him for one moment. "If I refuse to allow Sam to go with you, you'll fight for him?"

"If you leave me no alternative." Ignoring her gasp of fear, he moved to stand in front of her. "You've raised Sam since his mother died?"

"Yes."

"Giving up your own life."

Sam is my life. "I have my photography."

"You know what I mean."

Cassie breathed deeply through her nostrils, an edgy, jittery sensation in her belly. "Sam is enough for me," she said quietly. Her chin raised, shoulders squared.

His blue eyes deepened and he looked away from her to a distant private place, one in which she didn't belong. The moments ticked away—she counted them by the savage beat of her heart.

Suddenly his gaze connected with hers. He gave her a small tight smile. "I want Sam to know and love me as he does you."

"I don't trust you, Mr. Caine. I believe you intend to try to take Sam from me. But for now I'll play the game your way. Don't shove me too hard. My claws are sharp."

He laughed and dislike for him drenched her. "There's someone else to consider besides us."

"Who?"

"My mother."

Surprise surged through her. "Sam has a grandmother?"

He nodded. "She's gravely ill. She never really recovered from my brother's death. She's had one massive heart attack, and I've been told that another will—may kill her."

Cassie heard the give-away catch in his voice. "I'm truly sorry to hear that."

"She'll want to know her grandson."

Cassie sucked in a deep breath. "Does she know what happened between your brother and my sister?"

"She knows about the affair. That and his death were a shock to her. One she's never quite recovered from," he repeated.

How could she refuse Sam his grandmother? Or vice versa. She didn't want to hurt Mrs. Caine or deny Sam anything that would be good for him—give him extra love and stability that every child needed, but she didn't know these people. Knew nothing of them except what her sister had told her about Luke Caine and that was all bad.

Yet, much as she wanted to, she knew she couldn't outright refuse Joel Caine's pleas for Sam to know his father's family. There wouldn't be a court in Australia that would deny them access to Sam. She would have to place her trust in Joel Caine and hope they could work out something to suit them all.

She swallowed down the fear. Instinctively, she knew Joel Caine was not a man to be reckoned with. What he wanted, he'd go after with the same ferocity of a Bull Terrier for a rabbit. If he tried to take Sam from her, how could she fight him? He had money and he had power. Oh God, oh God, this was so darn awful.

She straightened her shoulders, tilted her head and said evenly, "And now you will tell her about Sam."

"Sam will be good for her." He smiled. "I can't begin to tell you what this will mean to her—knowing that Luke has a son, that she can meet him, hold him." He tilted his head. "My mother is a lonely woman, and time's not her friend. To see her grandson would give her immense pleasure." He nodded. "But then I'm sure you realize this."

Releasing a sigh filled with frustration and resignation, Cassie said, "And of course it's a given that I want what's best for Sam."

His eyes softened. "Then give Sam the chance to know his grandmother and me."

"You would want to take him to your home?"

"Yes."

"Where do you live?"

He lifted his shoulders. "Cattle station called Oriole. It's near a cattle town in the far north of Western Australia," he said. "About two hundred kilometers east of Derby."

Her head jerked. "Wouldn't you be teetering off the edge of Australia?"

He laughed. "You could say that. Oriole's a long way from city life."

She rolled her eyes. "Oriole. Named after the bird?"

"I'm surprised you know that. Not many do."

"I did a thesis at uni on Australian birds. While not actually going out and shaking hands with the birds, I got to know a lot about them and their habitat. The yellow oriole, if I remember correctly, is known for its superb call. A single bird may call continuously for more than half an hour from some leafy branch." She gave a soft laugh. "There endeth the lesson."

Before he could respond, she said, "And Oriole is Sam's inheritance?"

His smile was charming, well practiced. "Yes."

What if he decided to keep Sam? How would she fight him? Especially on his property. Who did you call for help in the outback?

Momentarily, a sense of sadness and fear engulfed her, then she gave herself a mental shake; she was a strong and capable woman with an strong sense of pride. Never would she allow anyone to see her frailties—least of all Joel Caine, brother to Luke, a man who lied and cheated without conscience.

All that was important to her was Sam and his welfare. The Caines were not only Sam's paternal family, they were, except for her, his only family.

"For how long?"

"A few weeks."

Her eyes widened. "Weeks!" she cried. "Are you completely mad? He's only four and never been away from me for more than a night. I can't allow him to go for weeks. That's too long for him. It's ridiculous to expect a toddler to be away from the only parent he's ever known to go live with strangers."

She drew erect. "He'll fret for me. He may not enjoy the visit and that may be upsetting for you and your mother. Besides I don't know you or your mother. It's too…"

She hesitated. She had wanted to say dangerous, but the word was too strong. "Radical a change for Sam. I'm sorry, but I can't allow it. You'll have to make other arrangements. Arrange for your visits here in Melbourne."

"That's impossible. I told you my mother is seriously ill. There's no way she could travel even a short distance. You must be reasonable, Miss Trenhaile."

"I'm trying to be just that, Mr. Caine," she responded. "And I agree Sam needs his father's family in his life, but to allow him to travel all that way without me is just not on.

"I'm not being perverse, Mr. Caine, I'm just trying to make it clear to you that Sam's welfare is most important to me—" She hesitated, then said, "As it is now to you, I'm sure."

His eyes grew thoughtful as she waited for his response. "What do you suggest, Miss Trenhaile?"

She briefly closed her eyes. *I suggest you take a long running jump from a short pier.* "I suggest I come with Sam." She wriggled her shoulders. "I don't want to spend weeks worrying about him, if he's fretting, if he's unhappy. I will accompany Sam until he's old enough to come on his own."

"He has to learn you can't be with him always," he reasoned, although his eyes had taken on a worried look.

Was this man completely devoid of common sense? She'd told him what she wanted and still he hedged around corners. "Can't you imagine how scared he'd be? Alone in a strange house with people he doesn't know? Of course he'll be frightened so far away from everything he knows and loves. You don't know him, Mr. Caine. What he likes, what he doesn't like. How he thinks that butterflies are angel's wings and how a storm terrifies him. That he doesn't like butter on his sandwich or oranges bring him out in a rash. Oh, there are so many things about Sam that you don't know."

"That's what I want to learn—all about Sam." His eyes lit up and a smile lifted the corners of his mouth. "Okay. Come with him. Meet my mother and that will waylay any doubts you may have. My mother will make you welcome."

"How do you know I'll be kind to your mother?" *Or that she'll be kind to me?*

He gave a wry grin. "I can imagine you being stubborn and headstrong but never vindictive."

She bit her lower lip to prevent from returning the smile. He had her down pat. "I suppose that's a sort of backhanded compliment." Hesitation, then, "There's my work. I'd have to put my work on hold." This was a big worry, as she had to meet the monthly rent, and there were electricity, gas, and telephone bills to pay.

"They told me at the gallery that your main work is for a healthy living magazine." He glanced around as if expecting sprouting organic fruit or home-grown vegetables.

"I photograph wholesome food. What to slap on the barbie that won't clog your veins and widen your hips. Things like that."

"Do you enjoy photographing sausages and chops?"

Was that a barb? Or was she over-sensitive to anything Joel Caine had to say? One thing she knew for sure, he annoyed the hell out of her and she'd take great delight setting him back on his heels. "It's okay. What I'd really like to do is to photograph the raw side of life."

"There's a raw side to the outback," he encouraged. "You'd find great subjects there. A different breed from city people."

The idea of outback men riding wild brumbies and lassoing rampaging beasts sat well with her, conjuring up images of rough-and-tumble, sexy men. Men like—her gaze flew to Joel's face. "How will you explain this to Sam? About me and his grandmother, I mean," he asked.

"Mr. Caine, I'll tell him the truth. Tell him that you've found him and want him to come to Oriole and meet his grandmother."

"Great, Cassie," he said, saying her name in a way that almost echoed intimacy. "That's great."

Her tongue probed her cheek. "How soon would we have to leave?"

"Day after tomorrow."

She nearly choked. "Day after tomorrow! Are you crazy? I can't be ready by then. There's so much to do. I have to pack and... and..." Her voice drained away. A strange almost giddy sensation overtook her, as if she'd been riding on an out-of-control merry-go-round for the past hour.

How quickly life could change. One moment she was sitting down to plan what to have for dinner and maybe she'd do the ironing tomorrow instead of today, and whammo, out of the blue steps the Evil King of the Outback intent on getting his own way, making abnormal things appear normal, and the hold she had on her life slipped a notch.

"You can handle this; or am I utterly wrong about you, and you fold in an emergency?"

She bristled as she noted his blue eyes twinkle impishly, fumbled for words, but defiance was her middle name. With a stubborn tilt to her head she said, "I can handle anything that comes my way."

Suddenly Joel towered over her. The sheer nearness of him stifled her, as if someone had cut off her air supply, and again she wished she'd met him under different circumstances. At a party, where they could have laughed and joked about the weather and he'd take her home, and she'd invite him in and let nature take its beautiful course.

This man's brother, Luke Caine, had started an affair with her sister while married to another woman, and then, when the truth was out, he had dumped Claudia, pregnant with Sam, without a backward glance.

Trust a Caine? She'd sooner put her money on a pit bull with a festered tooth.

She loathed the very idea of having anything to do with Joel and his family, but she loved Sam more, and if this was to be Sam's destiny, she'd do everything in her power to help him achieve it.

"Okay, it's set." He gave her a straight, intense look. "I'll see you the day after tomorrow. I'll be here, say, around eight. We have a long way to go. We need an early start." Their eyes connected. "Is that okay with you?"

"I'll be chomping at the bit."

He laughed. "I think I might enjoy having you around, Cassie."

"Gee, thanks. Now I'll cancel my subscription to need-friends-dot-com."

Walking across the room, she opened the door for him to leave, and closing the door firmly behind him, wiped the back of her hand over her forehead. Her skin was damp.

Treading quietly, she walked to Sam's bedroom, entered it, and looked down at the peacefully sleeping child. His mouth slightly open, long black lashes fanning cherub cheeks. She fingered the silk of his curls, touched the warmth of his skin. How she loved him, more than life itself.

She would sacrifice anything for her nephew's happiness—anything.

• • •

Joel stood facing the closed door, thinking about the woman inside.

Wow, was she stubborn and strong-willed. He'd have his hands full with her, that's for sure.

He turned and made his way down the steps and out onto the street. The pale evening sun came as a surprise. He had somehow expected it to be gloomy, overcast—raining even.

He hadn't expected any bonus from life, content in some strange way to live alone on the station—and now there was Sam. He had a nephew.

The joy had exploded inside his heart, and when he'd seen him and touched the gold of his hair, he knew then that he would do anything in his power to keep him happy.

Thinking about Sam made him remember another time, another place, and another life. The last night they had lain together—the night before their baby was born. Madeleine had spun away from him, grabbing the lower part of her stomach, and the first flash of fear entered him.

He remembered how he'd held his son to his chest when he'd cried his first breath and his wife had taken her last.

The pain of losing them had left Joel bereft and confused.

He had named his son Gabriel, after his father—it had seemed fitting somehow.

He'd buried his wife and son together and tried to get on with life; other people had lost their loved ones, but this offered him no solace as he had cursed the heavens for taking away his heart and leaving in its stead an empty shell.

Joel knew he would never love again. Never commit fully to another woman. He would never love another woman as much as he'd loved Madeleine.

He'd imagined no child would ever play in the dirt of Oriole. That he was last of the Caines.

And now there was Sam.

The pleasure at finding his nephew was absolute. It had been a long time since he'd experienced such deep emotion.

Now he had to tell his mother about Sam. And it had to be done gently. He didn't want to over-excite her with her bad heart. He had to prepare her, rather than turn up on the doorstep with a grandson she knew nothing about.

Joel reached his car, opened the driver side door, slid inside, and reached for his mobile phone. He dialed a number. "Queenie? Hi, it's me."

"Joel, is everything okay?" His mother's voice held a touch of concern.

"Yeah, everything fine, except—well, I have something to tell you."

"What is it, Joel?"

"It's good news. You have a grandson." He waited for her response, but the space between them crackled ominously. "Queenie—Queenie are you still there? Did you hear what I said?"

Her voice came out reedy. "I heard. Dear Lord, Joel. A grandson. I have a grandson? You have a son?"

He paused for a moment. "He belongs to Luke."

"Luke? I don't understand. Anne?" He heard the shock in the waver of her voice.

"No, not his wife. Claudia Trenhaile, the woman he'd met in Melbourne." He chewed his bottom lip. "I only found out about Sam by sheer luck."

"Why didn't he ever tell us about the baby?" Her voice cracked, full of emotion.

Joel understood his mother's emotional state. "He didn't know."

"Oh, this is all so tragic." Her sigh was deep. "Poor Luke. My poor, poor boy."

Her soft sobbing speared Joel's heart. "Queenie, are you okay?"

"Yes, yes." She sniffed. "How old is he?"

"Four."

A short, excited laugh. "Oh, Joel, have you seen him? What does he look like?"

He gave a small laugh. Delighted at his mother's excitement. "I saw him today. And he's the image of Luke."

"And his mother?"

"His mother is dead. He's being raised by his maternal aunt."

Claudia and Luke's affair filled his mind, and once again he cursed for not following through with his first instinct to see Claudia after Luke's death. They would have known about Sam right from the beginning. Sam could have grown up on Oriole. A cattle station was a good life for a boy. And if things turned out the way he planned, Sam would still have that life. All he had to do was convince Cassie. Of course he wouldn't deny her access to Sam, but Joel knew deep down inside he was doing what was best for Sam, and in some strange way for Cassie. Give her the chance to find a man to love and have children of her own.

"Oh, that poor girl. This is all so sad, Joel." He heard her quick intake of breath. "And his aunt has agreed to give him up?"

"No. I'm hoping to convince her that it's the best thing for Sam."

"Oh." The disappointment was evident in the long sigh coming over the phone. "What will happen, Joel? Will I see my grandson?"

"For the moment, we've worked something out." He hesitated, took a deep breath. "She's consented to bring him to Oriole."

"Then she'd allow us to have Sam from time to time?" The spark returned to her voice.

Hesitation. "She wants what's best for the boy, as we do."

"So she's a nice person?"

A picture of a slim, attractive, red-headed woman with eyes the color of crushed grass flashed into his mind. Yeah, she's real nice. "I'm sure you'll like her. Queenie, you have a grandson, be happy for that."

"What's his name?"

"Sam."

"Sam," she repeated softly. "What color is his hair?"

"What?"

"His hair, Joel. What color is it?"

"Like mine."

A soft sigh whispered over the phone. "Hurry home with my grandson."

"We'll be there as soon as possible."

Joel disconnected, throwing the phone on to the passenger seat. He pushed his head back into the soft leather. There was something about Cassie that distracted him deeply.

He had to remember how the affair between his brother and Claudia Trenhaile had affected his mother's life.

Now all he had to do was convince Cassie that Oriole was the best place for Sam. He gave a grim laugh. Not an easy task by any man's standard.

CHAPTER THREE

Cassie had barely slept thinking about the trip to Oriole. Being with Joel Caine. Meeting his mother.

And a more dire realization: Joel would never be out of her life. Sam was the solid connection between them.

Showered, she stepped into black lace bikini panties and matching bra, then sat on the edge of the bed and reached for her stockings. She leaned slightly over to stretch the beige-tinged nylon over one leg and then the other. Standing, she tugged the elastic tops until the stockings smoothed evenly over her legs.

She raised her eyes to the mirror. *Hell, I look like Dracula's sister after donating blood at the local Red Cross.*

She applied more make-up than normal, stood back, and surveyed the effect. She added a touch more eye shadow, another coat of mascara, and smeared her lips with a ruby gloss. A slight improvement. A gush of melancholic frustration overcame her. She strode to the window and opened it, let the cool air sweep across her burning face, and breathed in the scent of rose and jasmine. She heard the everyday sounds of people going to work; children's laughter and high-pitched chatter as they made their way to school.

Yet all these ordinary safe sounds did nothing to alleviate her doubts. Everything appeared abnormal to her, almost surreal, as if she was watching an animated scene from a Disney movie.

How could she be civil to the family of the man who had lied and cheated his way through life? And how could she bear to be with them for such a long time knowing this man had deserted her sister in her most desperate time? Of course the Caines would stick up for Luke and cast her sister in the light of seductress, a woman intent on taking another woman's man.

How would Mrs. Caine react if she said, "Your son was the cheat and liar; my sister thought him a single man; she imagined a life with him and their unborn child. It's your son who committed the sin, Mrs. Caine, not Claudia; not my sister."

She clenched her hands beneath her chin, trying to ease her thumping heart.

Yet with all this doubt and soul searching, Cassie knew she would go. Sam had the right to know his father's family. He had the right to be secure in the knowledge he had other people in his life besides her. He had an extended family that wanted to be an integral part of his life.

She knew they would fall in love with Sam; it was obvious that Joel had already lost his heart to his young nephew. And Sam would love them with the honesty and trust of a young child.

She couldn't—wouldn't—deny her nephew his father's family.

It wasn't forever. They would work something out to suit everyone.

She slipped on the dress she'd spread carefully across the back of a chair. It was a next-to-new dress with a full-flare mini skirt and high Chinese-neck collar; long, slim-fitting sleeves; and cinched waist. Cassie spun around, her eyes bulging. Chocolate fingerprints on the skirt. Sam's sticky fingers. Flying into the bathroom and wetting a facecloth, Cassie wiped the offending marks, finally getting most of the chocolate stain out. Big sigh. "It'll have to do."

She returned to her bedroom, moved to the dressing table, and reaching for her ruby stud earrings, she secured them into the lobes of her ears.

Slipping her feet into black leather high-heel shoes, she ran a comb through her hair, and swept it high, securing it with a strip of green satin ribbon. Okay, so she was overdressing, but she needed a boost to her self-esteem, and hadn't her mother always said it's better to dress up than dress down?

A splash of Trésor by Lancôme—her preferred scent, possessing a blend of lilac and apricot—and she was ready.

She glanced at the clock. Eight-forty-five. Hurriedly she finished packing her clothes into the case, closed it, and took it through to the lounge to sit next to Sam's.

Sam was still at the window where she had left him twenty minutes ago. Standing on a chair, his nose flattened against the glass, his hands pressed firmly on the windowsill. He had been back and forth from the window ever since she'd told him about his uncle, his newly found grandmother, and their trip to Oriole, repeatedly asking her the same questions in his childish impatience.

He'd accepted everything so simply. She'd explained that his uncle had been away in the outback and now he was back and wanted to know Sam. Sam had asked question after question and she'd done her utmost to answer them all. At last he was content and accepted the fact that his father's family had returned to him.

Cassie moved into the kitchen and, standing at the door, went through a mental checklist. Perishables disposed of. Windows locked. Trash removed. Dishwasher emptied. She turned and faced the lounge room. All electricity switches turned to the off position.

Everything, as far as she could ascertain, was in order for their departure.

She walked across the room to the telephone resting on a small table and did what she'd been putting off until she could put it off no longer. She dialed Jane's number.

"Hi, it's me."

"Hi, me. Why the early morning call?" Her voice took on an urgent tone. "Jeez, Cassie, nothing's wrong with Sam, is there?"

"No, Jane, no," she hastened to reassure her friend. "He's fine."

"Whew! Had me going there for a minute. Okay, what's up? You want a loan and think I'm your only friend with money?"

Cassie laughed. "You're the only friend I've got, period. It's not money."

"Okay, I'll bite, what is it?"

Cassie swallowed back the lump in her throat. "You'll never guess who turned up here at my apartment."

"Hmm, let me try. Johnny Depp. He's coming to Australia to claim you as his. He read your beseeching letter in the discover-love-I'm-desperate dot com loop, and fell for your 'have a figure that Elle McPherson would kill for' line."

Cassie chuckled. "You idiot."

"Okay, who came to your apartment?"

"Sam's uncle."

A long heavy pause. "Who?"

"Joel Caine." Even saying his name did strange things to her insides.

She heard the soft intake of Jane's breath. "Did he now? And what did he want? Your furniture? Your jewelry? Your life?"

Cassie gave a small half-crazed laugh. "His mother is desperately ill and not expected to live. He wants us to stay on his cattle station for a few weeks. Allow Sam to get to know his father's family."

"And of course you told him where to get off," Jane retorted.

"I agreed."

"Are you completely crazy?" Jane cried. "Didn't his brother do enough damage to Claudia? You can't trust this man, Cassie. He's cut from the same cloth as Luke. He'll do anything to get what he wants."

"Get what he wants? What do you mean?"

"Sam. That's what I mean. He wants Sam. It's as plain as the wart on a witch's nose. Do you truly believe he wants to share Sam with you? Grow up, Cassie."

A sick slam in her gut as her suppressed fears came to the fore. Jane had expressed Cassie's doubts, reinforced them. Was this really an elaborate plot to get custody of Sam? "What can he do? I've raised Sam. I'm his mother in every sense of the word."

"Yeah, well the courts may see it differently now there's trusty Uncle Joel and sweet old grandmother Caine crocheting woolly rugs for the world's poor and undernourished, and both vitally interested in Sam's welfare. Things have a way of turning around before you know it."

"Jane, don't." Unease trickled through her. "You're scaring me." Then common sense prevailed. "Anyhow I'd probably win, and Joel would gain visitation rights. The worst scenario would be joint custody."

A deep sigh echoed down the line. "I'm just saying be careful. Keep your eyes and ears wide open. Can't you get out of this visit?"

"No. Not now. Joel won't be completely separated from his nephew, and I can't blame him. We want what's best for Sam. He needs to know his father's family. A protection if anything should happen to me."

"Happen to you?" Jane squawked. "What do you mean? That if you're run over by a truck there'll be no one to look after Sam? What about me—am I a phantom in the mist or something?"

"No, no," Cassie quickly appeased. "It's important for Sam to know his father's family."

"Okay, I'll accept that you're doing the right thing for Sam. Whereabouts is this cattle station of his?"

"Near Derby, in Western Australia."

"Could he be any further away if he tried?" Another sigh. "You may as well be on the moon."

She took a deep breath. "Jane, it's only for a short while."

Cassie and Jane had been friends since high school. Cassie had studied photography and Jane journalism. Two years ago Jane began her own magazine, *Healthy Living*, and offered Cassie a job freelancing, which Cassie had eagerly accepted. With her small home studio, plus Jane's work, she made a steady income.

"Is he hot?"

Cassie twisted the telephone cord around a finger. "Sort of."

"He's either hot or he's not, which is it?"

Cassie glanced over at Sam. He was still staring out the window. "Hot," she whispered.

"Hmm, interesting. Do you fancy him in bed?"

"No," she snapped and then cursed inwardly at her too hasty answer. To Jane, a give-away. "Just a sec, Jane. Sam, please go and get my handbag from my bed. Okay, love?"

He frowned. "I don't wanna. I want to stay here."

"Pretty please. For Aunty."

He grinned. "Okay, Aunty C," he said scampering off.

"Of course I don't want to go to bed with him," she said like a teacher explaining infinity to five-year-olds. "He doesn't appeal to me that way."

"Well don't, even if you want to. You'll give him the upper hand."

"Jane, it's not a contest."

"Oh, yes, it bloody well is. Fuck him and you're fucked."

Cassie struggled to change the subject. "How about Tom?" Tom was Jane's latest and she'd been going out with him longer than any other man that Cassie knew of. "Still going strong?"

"He yodels when he comes."

"He what—yodels?"

"Yeah, like hitting a high C. It scared the bejeezus outta me at first, but now I rather like it."

Cassie giggled, then the girls were laughing until their tummies cramped. "Don't, oh, don't," Cassie gasped. "It's too much for any working girl."

"Tell me about it."

Cassie drew in a stabilizing breath. "I'm taking my equipment with me. Are you interested in a photographic study of the outback?"

"What I'd like is studies of the men of the outback and, if possible, their women. Their work. The way they live. The way they play. What they eat and what they drink. Can you do that?"

A surge of excitement. She'd never considered doing anything but city work. But now the idea of photographing the rough-and-tumble lives of stockmen intrigued her.

Would Joel let her use him as the main study? She imagined him on the front of the magazine astride a horse, shirtless of course, well-worn tight jeans, shabby leather boots, Akubra hat tugged low over his eyes, oozing confidence and oh-so-sexy. Heat surged through her. *Oh, my God.* She shook the image from her mind before it seared permanently.

"Consider it done."

"Good luck, Cassie. I'll email you every day."

"Yeah, don't I know it."

Jane chuckled. "Look after yourself. If you get into any sort of trouble or these people give you a hard time or even breathe too heavy around you, then give me a loud yell—I'll be there with my kicking-in-the-arse boots on." They disconnected.

Sam came back inside the room and, racing to her side, placed her handbag on her lap. "Here it is, Aunty."

"Good job, love," she said, leaning over and placing a kiss on his cheek. "You're the best boy ever."

Cassie stood and moving across the room slumped into a large, rather well-worn leather armchair, selected a magazine, and idly flipped through the pages, but she couldn't concentrate; the words were a blurred mess, the pictures meaningless blobs of color. She leaned her head back against the softness of the seat and stared vacantly at the ceiling. There in the left-hand corner was a spider web; *mental note, use feather duster more often.*

Without turning his face away from the window, Sam asked, "What time will he be coming, Aunty C?"

"Soon. He'll be here soon," she murmured, trying to summon up a smile. "I expect he has a lot to do. You know, sweetheart, like arranging for our luggage and stuff to be taken to Oriole."

He faced her. "Is he too late, Aunty C?" His sweet little face setting into clouded lines.

"Hey, sweetheart," she soothed, "he's only a little bit late."

"He's taking too long." He pouted.

"We'll be going to Perth by plane." She spoke to take his mind off Joel's late arrival.

His eyes widened. "A big plane? Like on television?"

"Uh huh. Sure will be exciting, don't you think?"

He turned away from her, back to his vigilance by the window.

"And from Perth Airport—well, I'm not too sure how we'll get to Oriole."

He turned slightly toward her. "Is Oriole a long way from Perth, Aunty C?"

"As I understand it, a rather long way."

"And Perth's not in Melbourne?"

"No, sweetheart. Perth is in Western Australia and Western Australia is big enough to hold Victoria, New South Wales, and still have room left for more."

His eyes grew rounder as he clapped his tiny hands. "Then Oriole must be real big."

"I'm sure it's the biggest."

He pressed his face against the windowpane, his voice so forlorn her heart ached. "Maybe he got lost or something?"

She smiled. "Maybe he had trouble starting his car or something?"

And when Sam faced her this time he was grinning. He moved away from his station at the window and, jumping down from the chair, came to her side. Leaning his elbows on her leg, he cupped his chin in his hands, and looked earnestly up into her eyes. She ran her fingers through his soft blond curls.

"Or maybe he missed the train."

She lifted him onto her knee. "Hmm, maybe. Or just maybe he decided to take a walk, seeing it's such a nice day."

"And maybe," Sam said, getting into the spirit of the game, "he decided to ride his bike and it got a hole in the tire."

"Or maybe he stopped to have a ride on the swings and slides in the park."

"Or maybe..." Both looked up at the sound of the front doorbell.

"It's him! It's my Uncle Joel from Oriole," yelled Sam, jumping off her knee and running wildly to answer the door before she could stop him.

Cassie stood, nervously twisting the sleeve of her dress into a tight knot. This was the moment she'd been dreading. She'd been hoping for a miracle. That perhaps Joel might have had second thoughts about bringing them to Oriole, but deep down she knew she'd been grasping at straws.

The very idea of facing him again made her damn nervous— Joel was too sexy for her peace of mind. And there was that dire thought of Jane's: that Joel wanted Sam permanently on Oriole.

Sam swung the door wide open. Man and boy stared at each other. At the sight of Joel, Cassie's heart went into fast-forward. Okay, so he was sexy and a hunk of a man, but that's as far as her interest went. The only thing between them was Sam, and that's all folks.

"Hi, Sam," Joel said.

Shy now, Sam said, "Hello." He looked down at his feet, scuffing the carpet with the sole of one red and white sneaker.

Joel knelt down in front of Sam, and took his tiny hand gently inside his, rubbing his thumb over Sam's knuckles.

• • •

Joel was unreasonably nervous. All night he'd been thinking, what if the boy didn't like him? What if he refused to come to Oriole? What if Cassie had changed her mind?

Now he stared into eyes the same color as his own and a fierce love for this little boy gripped him. "Great to meet you, Sam." He glanced at Cassie and gave her a small tight smile. "Did your aunt tell you who I am?"

"Yep," Sam declared and briefly looked at his aunt. "I mean yes," he corrected and Joel grinned.

She moved closer to Sam. "I wasn't sure what you wanted Sam to call you."

"Whatever he wants." He looked down at the boy, and from behind his back, Joel drew forth a Buzz Lightyear doll. "Here's someone who wants to get to know you, Sam, just like I do."

Sam's eyes rounded at the sight of one of his favorite cartoon character. "It's Buzz." He turned to Cassie. "Aunty C, look, it's Buzz!" He punched his fist into the air. "To infinity…and beyond," he yelled.

"That's great, Sam," Cassie agreed. "What do you say to your uncle?"

Sam jumped up and down on his toes, clutching the doll to him, then added shyly, "Thanks, Un…um…"

"Uncle Joel," Cassie prompted.

"Uncle Joel," Sam repeated.

A thousand emotions zinged through Joel at the sound of Sam calling him Uncle Joel for the first time.

An intense determination to do everything possible for this little boy filled him. He'd be the perfect uncle, or as great an uncle as he could be. "You're welcome." Joel straightened as best he could while still holding Sam's hand.

He glanced at Cassie. She was young. She needed to live life. Find a man and have her children of her own. She'd see in the end that what he intended to do was the right thing for all of them. A sluice of self-righteousness. As if he were making a sacrifice for this woman and she in return, would drop to her knees in gratitude.

"He's been excited all morning." Cassie's tone was reprimanding and he mentally cringed.

She reminded Joel of his third grade school teacher, Miss Lemon, who evoked up your misdemeanors with one withering glare. Miss Lemon, Joel was sure, had a third eye—a see-all, know-all eye in the back of her head.

"He thought you weren't coming." She pressed her lips together.

He didn't need a road map to read the signs. He'd mucked up well and good. "I had some last minute business to attend to." Joel ran a hand around the back of his neck. "I'm sorry, I should have phoned and let you know I'd be late. Careless of me."

She raised an eyebrow, and it surprised him that his apology had surprised her. It cemented the fact that Cassie didn't think well of him. So what, he wasn't out to win favors, nor did he give a hoot in hell what she thought of him. She was part and parcel of Sam and, at the moment, he'd go along with that.

"Did you explain to your mother about Sam and me?" Her voice was courteous but distant. She tilted her head slightly.

"Yes."

"What did she say? How did she take the news?"

"A bit apprehensive but accepting." Better than he'd expected, really.

Her expression stilled and grew serious. "Only natural, I suppose."

"Don't worry. It'll be okay."

She shrugged, and said offhandedly, "So you keep telling me."

...

Cassie's stomach still jangled with nerves, unsure of what to expect. Sure, Joel looked decidedly handsome in designer jeans and a blue-and-white checked cotton shirt. He had pheromones to squander.

He wore a loose jacket of dark blue. His blond hair was slicked back from his forehead and held with a soft gel. He looked as if he had just stepped out of a shower.

He moved nearer to her with his handsome face and brooding eyes, and the powdery smell of bath-soap mixed with the citrus odor of his cologne assailed her nostrils.

In one breathtaking moment she imagined his mouth crushed against hers. What he would taste like? Held safe in his arms, her body caressed by those strong, work-callused, sun-brown hands.

A woman would never forget him; he'd linger in her heart long after he'd left her. Once loved by Joel Caine, all other men would fade into insignificance as if they had never existed.

His lethal blue eyes connected with hers and she thought that her head might spin with dizziness if she held his gaze too long. Her heart slammed against her breast. Her cheeks and body heated in unison.

Wow, what was happening here? Sexual fantasies in the morning? *Get a grip, girl. He'll take you to his bed in a microsecond and leave you just as fast—the same as his brother had done to Claudia.*

Love 'em and hurt 'em was the Caine brothers' motto.

With the power of sheer will, she held his gaze, but her insides quivered like a bowl of jelly.

"Feeling all right about things?" he asked as if he were inquiring about her health and not their impossible arrangement.

"It'll be okay."

"I'll try to make it as pleasant as possible."

"Don't worry about me. I'll just blend in with the scenery. You won't even know I'm there."

He chuckled. "I doubt that. I think you'll make your presence well and truly known." He looked around. "Should I get in anything special for Sam?"

Her voice rose in surprise. "Special?"

"Food. What he likes to drink." He shrugged and grinned. "Don't know much about kids."

"He has an allergic reaction to citric fruits, and I don't allow him peanuts, not yet, not until he's over seven. Otherwise he eats what everyone else does."

"I ordered some toys this morning to be delivered to Oriole. Hope he likes them."

"You shouldn't have troubled."

That irritating smug look on his face made her palm itch. "Nothing much. A tricycle. Paints, books, planes, and cars. Boy toys. No biggie."

Sam tugged his uncle's jeans. "Are you really my uncle?"

Joel scooped the boy into his arms, holding Sam away from him, studying the boy's face as eagerly as Sam was studying his. "Yes, I am."

Cassie noticed a muscle clench in Joel's jaw. *He's nervous.* A faint flutter of compassion for him.

"My daddy's in heaven with my mummy," he said so solemnly that her heart broke.

Joel nodded. "I'm your daddy's brother."

The boy chewed his bottom lip. "Did you live with my daddy when you were little?"

"Sure did. And when we get to Oriole there's a lot of things of your dad's I can give you. And your grandmother will tell you stories about him, too." He drew the child into his body. Sam looked so tiny, or was it because Joel was so big? "Is that okay with you, Sam?"

Time stood still. Cassie's heartbeat had been placed temporarily in storage as she waited for Sam's response. If he didn't like it, Sam would say so. In all his life, the boy had never told a lie. Even when caught out in a mischievous act, Sam told the truth, and she'd encouraged him in his truth telling.

The silence was suffocating.

"Did you go away to the outback and forget you had me?" Sam asked.

"I was sad for a long time and didn't want to see anyone, but now I want to be your uncle."

Sam titled his head. "Why are you sad?"

"Because I couldn't be with you."

Sam nodded, as if in understanding. "And now you're gonna be with me."

Joel touched Sam's cheek with his fingertips. "For the rest of your life, if you'll let me."

Sam threw his arms around Joel's neck, and planted a wet sloppy kiss on his cheek. "Yep, that's fine with me, Uncle Joel."

"Me too, Sam." Joel's voice was husky, and his eyes became the deepest blue.

Cassie's breath exhaled in a gush. She felt relief at the rapport between Joel and Sam. Although with the powerful aura of natural charm that surrounded Joel, it was difficult not to respond to him.

"Sam's never been out of Victoria," she said. "He's never been on a plane, so all this is a big first for him."

"Then I'll have to make it as exciting as possible," Joel said, holding the boy closer to him. "So he'll remember his first trip to Oriole for the rest of his life."

She gave a soft laugh. "I don't think it's something he'll easily forget."

She had wanted to say, "It's you he'll never forget. You are his uncle and in the space of a few minutes, you have become vitally important to Sam and his life."

"Aunty C said kangaroos live at Oriole," Sam said, vying for his uncle's attention.

"Sure are, Sam. There are lots of animals roaming free in the outback. Are you pleased to be coming?"

Sam nodded his head, his curls tumbling over his forehead. Joel placed a kiss on his rosy cheek. "Then let's get going, Tiger."

"I'll get his coat and hat," Cassie said walking over to the chair. She picked up a pale blue parka and a blue and white beanie. She returned, reaching out to take Sam from Joel's arms.

Joel shook his head and took the clothing from her. "I'll do it."

Standing the boy on the edge of the table, Joel rather awkwardly helped Sam into his coat. Sam never stopped chattering while Joel dressed him. Joel arranged the hat in place.

"It's back to front." She spoke quietly.

He threw her an inquiring glance. "What?"

She pointed. "His hat. You're putting it on back to front."

He grinned and her mouth responded automatically. "Hey, Tiger, I've got a lot to learn." He turned back to Cassie. "Is he okay now?"

She smiled shyly. "He's perfect."

"That's something we'll always agree on," he assured her. "Got everything you need?"

"Yes, I think so."

"Everything locked and secure?"

"Yes, everything."

Hoisting Sam high on his shoulders, Joel marched him toward the door.

"Uncle Joel," he cried.

Joel stopped dead in his tracks. "What's wrong, Tiger?"

"I forgot Buzz."

"Can't go without Buzz Lightyear."

"He'd be sad, wouldn't he, Uncle Joel?"

"Too right, Sam."

Joel marched them backwards, bent down, and flipped the doll upward into Sam's eager hands, and again strode purposely toward the front door. Stooping, he hoisted up the larger of the suitcases, glanced over one shoulder, and said, "Manage the other one?"

She nodded.

"Duck your head, Tiger," Joel said, and left.

Cassie couldn't explain the feeling that was now engulfing her. Trepidation fluttered in her throat and she swallowed harshly, waylaying the emotion before it took hold of her and she reneged on her pact to go with Joel.

It's all for the love of Sam.

It was more now than her fear of the unknown and what may be waiting for her at Oriole. It was Joel and the conflicting emotions he was wringing from her. It was all so illogical, and yet somehow so right.

Confusion mingled with fear.

All she had to do was to remain remote from him. Keep on her side of the fence.

I can do this.

Yet as she looked at his fast retreating back, Cassie despaired, found she couldn't move.

Joel called, "Come on, Cassie."

"Come on, Aunty C," Sam's voice echoed.

She picked up the suitcase and grabbed her coat and handbag from the back of a chair and made her way out of the apartment to the waiting taxi, Joel, and whatever waited for her at Oriole.

CHAPTER FOUR

They boarded the plane at Tullamarine. Cassie, thinking Sam would enjoy sitting with his uncle, sat in the seat behind them, but was nearby if Sam needed her.

Joel hadn't spoken more than five words to her since they had left her apartment and on the long drive to the airport. Sam had clung to his Uncle Joel refusing to leave his side.

Why was she beginning to feel like an alien from the planet Zora?

Everything had happened too fast. She'd had no time to think things through carefully enough.

Joel lifted Sam from his seat and on to his knee pointing to something interesting outside.

Sighing deeply, she studied the interior of the plane with commendable interest, but it was only outwardly that she appeared rational and unruffled; inside she was a screaming nut case.

She stared at the back of his head. Joel really had gorgeous hair. The special way it curled around his collar, and with those blue eyes and tanned skin, he looked like an advertisement for a health magazine.

Eat Zippy Beans and you too can end up with a body like mine.

Although you'd need more than Zippy Beans to create a body like Joel's. His had come from working outdoors—sheer manual labor.

Images of Joel branding cattle, bending horseshoes with his bare hands, riding bareback through thick bushland on a wild brumby flashed into her mind. A *Man from Snowy River* image.

She squirmed. *Damn, he's not that great.* She'd known sexier men, more virile men, hadn't she? She strained her brain—it had been a

42

long time between men. *Concentrate. Yes, got him. Steve Branshaw, a hunk of a man* …except he was gay, she sighed. *Okay, okay, let's think. Got it, Paul.* Paul Sheffield, the perfect lover, except she'd discovered he'd had a harem of women planted around Melbourne. Bugger. Maybe if she appraised Joel more dispassionately. Heck, he wasn't that handsome, his nose was slightly crooked, and his hair far too long. Okay, his eyes were an impossible shade of blue. Many men had blue eyes, but his were different somehow—much more vivid, much more intense. They reminded Cassie of a painting by an Old Master where the eyes fixed on you and followed you around. No matter where you were in the room, you couldn't get away from the disturbing gaze.

She tugged the high collar of her dress. She'd noticed the way women stared at him at the airport, as if he was the best thing since sliced bread. Not that she cared in the least, let them stare as long as they wanted. Let them have him if they dared.

A voice penetrated Cassie's thought. She glanced up, stared vacantly at a flight attendant, then realized she was speaking to her. Blinking Cassie said, "Excuse me?"

"Is there anything I can get you? A drink perhaps. Coffee, tea?"

"No. No thanks."

Cassie looked out of the window, wishing she had bought a mystery novel at the airport—anything to take her mind off Joel.

The calm voice of the pilot came over the intercom. "We'll be landing at Perth Airport in a few minutes. We hope you've enjoyed your flight with Qantas."

At the flash of the fasten-your-seat-belt sign, she buckled up and prepared for landing.

CHAPTER FIVE

Joel had booked them into a five-star motel not far from the airport. It would be too long a trip for Sam and her to do in one hit, he'd explained. Best they stay the night here in the motel and get an early start in the morning.

Joel unlocked the door with the magnetic key, and the porter hoisted their luggage inside the suite. Cassie ushered Sam inside the room. Joel tipped the young man and closed the door after he'd left.

"Where should I put your bags?" he asked Cassie.

"Next to the bed, thanks."

He did as she bid, handing her the key. Cassie smiled her thanks. "Anything else you need?"

"No, everything's—" she was going to say perfect, but changed her mind and said, "here that I need."

"Order anything you want from room service."

"Sure."

"I want Sam—" he hesitated as if she were an afterthought and said, "and you to have everything you need and want."

She bit back the word "peachy." "Thanks."

"Well, I better get going."

"Yeah, you'd better."

He nodded and chuckled. "Want to do a bit of sightseeing while we're here?"

"Thanks, but no. I'm bushed." She glanced down at Sam. "And so is Sam."

"Okay, have a few hours rest, and I'll take you and Sam to dinner."

She smiled warmly. "Sounds great," she said, resisting the impulse to tell him she'd prefer to eat with Sam in their room, because she knew that Joel wouldn't understand the reason behind her need to be alone.

He gave her a brief nod and walked briskly away.

Cassie hadn't had time to think, to breathe easily, since Joel had come barging into her life: without warning, decidedly uninvited, and most assuredly unwelcome.

"Why can't Uncle Joel sleep with us?" Sam demanded.

"He has to have his own room." She ruffled his curls.

"But why?"

"Because."

"'Cos why?"

She sighed. "Because he's an adult, and adults like their own space." His bottom lip trembled and Cassie soothed him with, "He's taking us out to dinner."

His eyes sparkled. "McDonald's?"

"I hope not," she muttered. She looked around the suite. The main room consisted of a bedroom-cum-sitting room with the décor of a five-star motel. A door to the right led to an adjoining bedroom; she guided Sam to this room. "This is your room, Sam." She lay on top of the bed.

"Come here, baby." He crawled on the bed beside her. She undressed him down to his T-shirt and underpants. Kicking off her shoes, and with a grateful sigh, she fell back on the bed. Sam cuddled into her. She drew the cover over their legs. She looked down to say something to him, but he was asleep. Smiling, she curled into her nephew's warmth and within minutes followed Sam into a blissfully sound sleep.

• • •

A rap on the door awoke her with a start. It had grown dark outside. They must have been asleep for hours. "Who is it?" she called, while knowing full well who it was and what he wanted.

"It's me," Joel called back. "Are you ready for dinner?"

"Give me half an hour, okay?"

"Everything okay?" he asked, his voice quiet, demanding.

She pressed her lips together. "Everything's fine."

"Have a sleep?"

She rolled her eyes. "You woke us."

She heard the shuffle of his feet outside her door. "Sorry. Thought you'd be getting hungry."

"I'm getting hungry, Uncle Joel," Sam yelled as if Joel were in the next state and not outside their door.

"Then hurry up, Sam," he encouraged, "and we'll get something good to eat."

She pressed her hand across her eyes, and sighed deeply. "Half an hour," she repeated.

A moment's hesitation, as if he were reluctant to leave, then, "I'll go to the bar and have a beer."

"Come on, Sam," she said, encouraging her nephew to move. "Let's have a quick shower and get changed into some clean clothes."

Twenty minutes later, they were dressed and waiting for Joel. He knocked on the door a few minutes later.

He took them to the motel restaurant. Joel ordered a steak rare, mashed potatoes, and green beans, while Cassie had a Greek salad and Sam a cheeseburger and fries.

Everything had been going well. The meal was excellent, with white linen tablecloths and silver service. The conversation, although stilted, was at least polite.

"What have you in mind for Sam's education?"

"Excuse me?" she said, surprised again by this unpredictable man.

"His schooling," he said. "Where did you plan to enroll him?"

She raised her chin with a cool stare in his direction. "I hadn't given it much thought. I'd imagined the local primary."

His eyes were compelling, mesmerizing. "I meant when he's ready for higher education."

She shrugged. "High school, and if he's smart enough, university."

He frowned, his eyes level under drawn brows. "I'd like him to go to Timbertop."

She took a quick breath of utter astonishment. "Didn't Prince Charles of Wales go to school there?"

"Yeah, that school."

"Why?"

"I want him to have the best."

A warm glow fused through her. That Joel wanted the best education for Sam didn't surprise her, but it pleased her. It was something that she'd never be able to afford. "That's wonderful, Joel."

"Derby has a fine School of the Air."

She stiffened. "Has it now. And what is School of the Air exactly?"

"It's a generic term for correspondence schools for the primary and early secondary education of children in remote and outback Australia. In these areas, the school-age population is too small for a conventional school to be viable."

"Are you suggesting that Sam stay with you?" Her fears, her anxieties joined hands and did a war dance. She'd been right from the beginning. Joel intended to keep Sam whether she liked it or not. Who did he think he was? With his scowl. His brooding eyes and his macho swagger. She had news for the illustrious Joel Caine and it was all bad.

"You think Sam should stay with you?" she repeated. She looked straight at him, very direct, very candid, and very composed.

"Will I be going to School of the Air, Aunty C?"

"I'm not sure, Sam. Uncle and I are discussing which is best for you."

"I merely mentioned the School of the Air and how good they are."

"Why?"

Her reaction seemed to amuse him. "Why what?"

Infuriating man. "Why mention the school at all?"

"Thought you'd be interested."

Artful man. "I'm not."

"Are you and Uncle fighting? Cos I want to go to School of the Air, don't I?"

"We're not fighting, Sam," Joel said. "We are, as your aunty says, discussing the best schools for you."

Her tongue rolled around her cheek. "Sam lives with me."

"When I go to school I'll be a big boy then, won't I, Uncle Joel?"

"Sure will, Sam. Have to buy you bigger boots."

The boy stretched out a leg. "Can I have cowboy boots, Uncle Joel?"

"Sure can, Sam. The best boots I can find."

"Finish your dinner, Sam. There's a good boy," Cassie said.

Joel reached over and gently touched the top of her hand. An electrical charge raced up her arm. "Did I say thanks?"

She was barely able to hold back her gasp of surprise. She was finding it difficult keeping up with him. "What?"

He flashed an irresistibly devastating grin, which she was thankful left her cool and in control. Okay, her heart was a trifle out of control, but that was through their unnerving conversation and nothing to do with the man.

"Thanks for making things so easy for Sam and me."

She looked at him with amused wonder. "It's okay."

His fingers were tracing lazy circles over her knuckles. She trembled. The heat of his fingers scorched her hand—it gathered momentum and raced up her arm and entered her body at the speed of light. Oh so wonderfully warm and alive. And the colors

48

of the restaurant took on a deeper hue, the lights brighter and the people around them more energetic and animated. Going to bed with Joel would be exciting. Hell, she was excited at the mere thought.

"I'll do my best to make your stay with us happy." Before she could reply, he said, "Want some ice cream, Sam?"

"Yes, please."

"Aunty C?" said Joel with a grin.

Why couldn't she resist him? "Yes, please."

CHAPTER SIX

Joel carried the sleeping boy inside his room and placed him gently on the bed. Together they undressed him and, leaving him in his underpants and T-shirt, covered him with a cotton blanket, as it was so much warmer here in the west than at home.

"He should sleep soundly 'til morning," she whispered as they walked into the adjoining room, leaving the bedroom door slightly ajar.

Joel looked at her and she melted under his candid stare. "I enjoyed tonight," he said.

"Me too."

"It's been a long time since I was—well, normal I guess. My mother's sickness. Running the station, it takes its toll. You forget to relax. Look at the stars, smell the flowers, read a good book. I eat on the run. Getting up at dawn and falling into bed each night exhausted. It's great to slow down. Enjoy the simple pleasures of life." He grinned and she sucked in a quick breath.

"Thanks, Cassie."

"Hey," she said completely embarrassed but secretly so pleased she could burst. "No biggie."

His eyes were dark and unfathomable. "I can't begin to tell you what he means to me."

"I have some idea."

He shook his head. "No, I don't think you do." He moved in on her. *Give me air.* The room was stifling. Had the air-conditioner broken down? "I need to do things for him. I need to be a part of his life—an important part." He hesitated. "Do you understand what I'm saying?"

"Yes," she whispered, wishing he wouldn't stand so close. Close enough that she could see the tiny crinkles around his eyes. Close enough that her eyes slightly crossed with the effort of trying to hold his gaze.

"You've so lovely," he said softly.

"Me, lovely. Don't think so."

"I think so."

Joel placed an arm around her waist, and dragged her closer to his body. His heat. And suddenly an overwhelming desire swamped her and she wanted him to touch her, desire her. She wanted desperately to feel the pressure of his mouth against hers.

She offered little resistance as she fell against his body, and felt the hardness of his chest against the softness of her breasts. An indescribable feeling enveloped her. It was at once wonderful and scary. Wonderful because it alerted every nerve cell in her body, had them singing for his touch, making her want to join with this man in the most primitive of ways, and scary because she couldn't handle it.

I'm going to kiss him.

I don't want to do this.

Yes, I do.

She stood on tiptoes and flicked her tongue beneath his chin.

He kissed her, hard and long. Hot kisses went from the curve of her cheek to her throat. Her hand found its way beneath his shirt. She felt breathless at the warm solid feel of him.

His tongue caressed her parted lips. She trembled as the tip of his tongue probed deep and awakened a desire that surged through her like a tidal wave. Her need burned deep inside her.

They broke free, breathing heavily.

His hand tangled in her hair, and he whispered her name so softly. Had she imagined the lulling sound of his voice?

He kissed the hollow of her neck. An uncontrollable excitement deep down inside her as his hand came to lightly brush her breast through the soft material of her shirt.

"Cassie, Cassie," he whispered. "You taste so damn good."

With a soft groan, he kissed her again and she returned his kiss with equal abandonment.

His hands slid down her back and clasped her buttocks. Pulling her rock solid against him, she rotated and pushed against his hardening erection.

His name came out on a whispered breath.

He threw her on top of the bed. His hand squeezed her breast. She closed her eyes and floated somewhere between heaven and earth. His touch made her throb. Desire swamped her. She wrapped a leg around his hip. His mouth was hot and demanding. He twisted her so that she was laying on top of him now.

Her need was so great that she wanted to sacrifice the foreplay, tear the clothes from their bodies, and have him enter her.

Hurry, hurry.

His fingers groped under her shirt and yanked the hooks of her bra. Her fingers matched his. She tugged his shirt free from his jeans, and ripped it open. Buttons popped and flew through the air like self-propelled missiles.

In the other room, Sam gave a moan and stirred in his sleep.

It was as if a fire alarm had gone off.

Scrambling to their feet, Cassie fumbled to hold on to her bra, crunching her shirt in front of her.

Joel looked abashed and mighty uncomfortable with his shirt hanging loose and his mouth smeared with her lipstick.

"Damn, what happened?"

Like she knew?

Her cheeks burned as humiliation flooded her. "Please go," she croaked. Her legs felt deboned; she could barely hear him for the thudding of her heart.

"Cassie, please—"

"I said, go."

With the dignity of a queen at a royal sitting, she moved to the door. Still clutching her shirt, she opened the door with her free hand and stood slightly back as Joel made his exit.

He turned to her and said, "Cassie, I—"

"Goodnight, Joel." She drew to her full height and held out her hand. "And thanks for a lovely evening."

Lovely evening? Was she completely insane? His ruined shirt hung from his body like a flag on a windless day. She was practically naked and she was thanking him for a lovely evening.

My heavens, they had just romped on top of the bed like teenagers with raging hormones, and now she wanted him to shake her hand. She's known this would happen—that given half a chance he'd send her around the bend.

He took the proffered hand and shook it as if closing a business deal. "Good night, Cassie. I'll see you around six? Is that okay with you?"

Go, please go. She eased her hand from his tenacious grip. "Yes, that's fine."

"We can have breakfast together."

I'll never eat again. "I think it best if I order breakfast in our room," she dismissed and seeing the look of disappointment quickly appeased him with, "it will give Sam that extra sleep time he'll need."

"Okay. I'll knock at six-thirty."

Go, damn you, go. She closed the door and wondered what had happened. She'd lost control so easily. She'd actually attacked Joel like some desperado that hadn't had sex for—damn, she *was* a desperado that hadn't had sex for years.

What did he expect, coming on to her that way?

Or had she come on to him?

She took a vow here and now that it certainly would not happen again.

Like an accomplished girl guide, she was now well and truly prepared.

CHAPTER SEVEN

They were dressed and ready to go by six fifteen.

She wore a Bonds cotton opera top and an Akira Isogawa bias cut silk mini skirt and taupe stockings with her very high-heeled sandals. Her hair tied in a high ponytail with hair elastic, wrapping pieces of the ponytail around the elastic in different directions and fixed with grips. She sprayed hairspray to hold the style in place.

She wore a minimal amount of make-up, applying a smear of Angel Red lipstick.

They were watching an in-house video of *The Lion King* when Joel knocked at six thirty. They greeted each other cordially, each trying not to make eye contact.

"Sleep well?" he asked her.

"Like a baby," she replied.

Liar, liar. She'd tossed and turned all night. Humiliation and a bizarre yearning playing a game of set and match inside her.

"And you?" she asked with the civility of a hostess inquiring about a guest's comfort.

"Never heard a thing from the time my head hit the pillow." He entered the room. Sam rushed to greet him. He lifted the boy into his arms. "Ready to go to Oriole, Tiger?"

"Yep. Uncle Joel?"

"Yes?"

"Aunty C was crying in the bathroom, weren't you, Aunty C?"

Her cheeks flashed heat as humiliation washed through her. "Sam!" Horrified that Joel could have the slightest suspicion about how she truly felt about what happened last night. She stared at

Joel almost pleading with him to understand and not laugh at her. "I…I wasn't. I had a sniffle."

"Cassie, about last night. I'd really like you to know that—"

"Sam, have you got everything?" she interrupted. She didn't need Joel apologizing for last night. That would be the humiliation to end all humiliations. Let her imagine he'd desired her as a woman, and carried no regrets at all.

"Yes, Aunty C."

"Then let's go," she said. Taking him from Joel's arms and placing the child on his feet, she marched Sam out of the motel suite head high, purpose in her stride as if last night had never happened. As if she hadn't ripped the shirt off Joel's back in her longing to have him make love to her.

It'll be all right. Once we're at Oriole there'll be other people. They wouldn't be alone and temptation wouldn't dangle its dangerous lure in front of her, and she'd be able to resist Joel.

CHAPTER EIGHT

They made their way across the tarmac, veering left to another much smaller airfield where they boarded a red twin-engine Beechcraft. It was only when Joel settled them into their seats that Cassie realized he was to fly it. Her heart rehearsed a rumba.

Two things scared Cassie senseless. One was flying in light aircraft, and the other was snakes. She'd rather have root canal work done on all her teeth than fly in this plane—a plane that, to her eyes, didn't look stronger than one of Sam's toy planes.

"Are you a seasoned pilot, Joel?" she asked as he strapped Sam into the seat beside him and Cassie into the seat behind him.

"I've flown before."

"Before. Before what?" Her voice was lightly laced with fearfulness.

"Relax, Cassie," he said with a wink like they were sharing some secret. "You're going to enjoy this."

"Since when have you had me down as a masochist?"

He laughed. "You've got to learn to loosen up, take a chance on life."

"I prefer reading and bedroom slippers by the fire and the mind-lulling certainty that I'll wake up in my bed with my head still connected to my shoulders."

Chuckling, Joel slid into the pilot's seat and fiddled with the controls. The engine thundered to life. A two-way conversation with the control tower and they were roaring down the tarmac. Then they were climbing as if intent on breaking the sound barrier.

A buzz took up in her ears and she swallowed harshly to clear the noise.

As a child, when things got too intimidating for her, Cassie would spell out words backwards, and, as the years passed and this became too easy for her in English, she did it with French words. "E-U-Q-S-E-N-A-M-O-R, E-T-I-L-A-U-X-E-S—"

"Did you say something?" Joel asked.

Her cheeks heated as she realized the words she had chosen. "No, I—"

The plane gave a lurch to the left. Apprehension caused her to reach out with her left hand and grab Sam's shoulder much harder than she had intended.

Sam flinched. "What, Aunty C?"

"How's things, Sam?"

"What things?"

They were flying a straight course now. Joel reached over and gently removed her vice-like grip from the boy's shoulder. He ruffled Sam's hair. "Don't worry about Aunty C, Sam, she's just being a girl."

To her sheer horror, Sam agreed. "Girl's are silly, aren't they, Uncle Joel?"

She forgot her fear as she flinched at Sam's response. What was this? When had the sudden rush of comradeship flared between uncle and nephew?

"Too right." Joel answered in a voice that hinted they were sharing a secret that didn't include her. *A wink and a nod and She'll be right, mate.*

A spirited, incisive reply sprang to Cassie's lips, but it was swallowed down in a gulp of fear as the plane tipped gently to one side. "Oh-h-h, is this a short trip?" she muttered through clenched teeth. Either Joel didn't hear or just plain wouldn't answer.

They flew in silence and she relaxed. It wasn't so bad and Joel really was a skilled pilot.

She was as safe as if she were travelling in a commercial flight. Perhaps better than a commercial flight because here she wasn't squashed next to another passenger and forced into holding a conversation or, worse still, have the person next to you fall asleep and use your shoulder as a pillow.

With the hum of the engine, the heat of the plane and the lack of sleep over the last few nights, Cassie's eyes grew pleasantly heavy. She must have nodded off until she heard Joel call to her. "Coongan River."

She forced her eyes to flutter open. "Marble Bar?"

He nodded. "Australia's hot spot. It averages in the high thirties Celsius even in the winter."

She looked down at the historic gold township.

"Gold was found in the late 1800s, and the population soared to five thousand. Now it's around three hundred."

"How do they manage to live there in all that heat?"

He lifted his shoulders. "You get used to it," he said. "Have you ever been to Derby?"

"Never. I've never been to the outback, although it's something I've always wanted to do." She pressed her tongue to her cheek. "I've read about the boab tree," she said, wanting to educate Sam—okay, wanting to impress Joel that she wasn't a complete ignoramus about the west, "and how its trunk resembles a bottle."

"There's a boab tree just outside Derby that's probably the most photographed curiosity in the northwest."

She pushed a fallen lock of hair back from her forehead. "I remember," she cried excitedly. "It's called the Prison Tree. It's reputed to have been used in the 1890s as a lockup for prisoners on their way to Derby for sentencing. I believe it's large enough to hold about a dozen people."

"That's right. And Sam, Aboriginals of the Mowanjum community carve ancient and intricate designs on boab nuts. I'll take you there so you can see it for yourselves," he said.

"Can we go tomorrow?" Sam said.

"Not tomorrow but soon," Joel answered.

"We've got a lot of wonderful things to see," Cassie piped in.

"And we've got lots of time to see them," said Joel.

He drew silent, and Cassie leaned her head back into the soft seat. How long did he expect them to stay at Oriole? She had to get back to her apartment and her job. And what would Joel expect once she returned home? They could work something out to suit them all, she was positive. She pushed back the resurfacing doubts that Joel wouldn't relinquish Sam so easily.

She was sticky and tired and desperately in need of a cool shower. Would this trip never end?

Why anyone would want to live permanently in the outback was beyond her imagination. She loved city life. She was comfortable with the hustle and bustle. Her lungs thrived on smog. She liked the shops, galleries, and theatres. She liked taking Sam for long walks through picturesque parks—neat and tidy with wooden seats and delicate flowers.

She glanced out of the plane window. The utter vastness of the west was amazing. She looked down. The plains were carpeted with the gold of everlastings and splashes of the red and pinks of boronia and leschenaultia. The flowering gums were a mass of red and the strange-looking felt-like native kangaroo paws invaded the plains. Lilies, banksias, parrot bush, flame peas, and native foxgloves were all displayed in a magnificent abundance, as if she could reach out and touch them.

It was beautiful.

She fell back against her seat, pushing her head adjacent to the head rest. How had all this had happened? How was it she was flying across Western Australia with Joel? To live with a man she barely knew on his outback cattle station.

Are you mental? Tell him you want to go home. Frustration fluttered in her throat. *It's not forever.* Only a few short weeks and then back to familiar and safe life.

The plane seemed to drone on forever, until finally Joel called to her. "Look down." Cassie craned her neck to see out of the side window. "A diamond mine."

Large craters cut deep into blue-tipped mountains. He flew lower and she could see ore-handling and processing equipment, and high-pressure roller crushers.

Interested, Cassie asked, "Is there still a large market for diamonds, Joel?"

"As long as there are women, diamonds will always be in great demand. I know the mine manager and he told me they have an expansion plan of one hundred million dollars. Their production rate is at present thirty-five million carats a year. The mine's producing highly prized champagne and cognac diamonds."

"It all sounds so—so rich."

His laugh was soft and pleasing. "Things still can go wrong," he said. "They have to be careful not to flood the market."

"Flood the market? What would happen then?"

"One famous result of flooding was rough diamonds being able to be stored unguarded in milk churns at a railway siding at Kimberley, in South Africa. They were simply not worth stealing." He pointed out of the window. "Look, Sam, see there. That's Oriole—we're home."

Sam bounced in his seat with excitement. "Are we going to land, Uncle Joel?"

"Soon."

Cassie peered out of the window. It was truly beautiful. The expanse of green and gold shimmered in the afternoon sun.

They were flying so low she could see the cattle and horses grazing peacefully. So many people and buildings that, to Cassie, it seemed like a small township.

"Are those your cattle?" she asked.

"Some of them. Most graze in the hills. We use a helicopter to round up the several thousand beasts waiting to be driven to the stockyards," he explained. "We have to move before the wet arrives. Downpours often follow a long spell of dry weather and submerge vast tracts of territory, and you don't need much imagination to realize the disruption it causes to transport and communications. It can turn the land into a huge reservoir."

He flew even lower and through a cloud of swirling dust she could make out the homestead. A magnificent two-storied structure erected high on a hill, and it surprised her that something so magnificent could be built so far from civilization.

At last their journey was over and Joel, after making a perfect landing, helped them from the plane. Sam raced on ahead, skipping and jumping as he stretched his muscles, delighted to be out of the restriction of the plane.

Cassie leaned against the plane endeavoring to regain some semblance of a stable calm state. After a few moments, her condition improved enough to take in her immediate surroundings.

The savage heat hit her in the face like a hot, wet towel. Beads of perspiration settled around her forehead and upper lip. Was she in a sauna?

Joel, who had moved on a few steps, turned and looked back at her. "You okay?" he called.

Cassie took a couple of paces toward him, but her legs were like jelly, and she rocked precariously in her shoes. He was at her side in less than instant, his arm encircling her waist.

His nearness disturbed her. More than she wanted to admit—more than possible. She searched for a word—bothered, that was it. Joel Caine bothered her.

"You'll find your land legs in a moment," he assured her as she moved away from his touch.

"I feel as if my legs are made of rubber," she said, but the strength was fast returning to her limbs.

She fumbled with the elastic in her hair, endeavoring to straighten the loose ends. It slipped loose and her hair fell in waves around her face and down over her shoulders. She imagined it looked scraggy and awful, but she was too tired to care. She slipped the elastic into the pocket of her handbag.

She gazed up into his eyes.

How extraordinary, I can actually see blue sparking lights in his eyes. I've never noticed that before.

Without warning, he moved in close. She became aware of his scent, a musky male smell of eucalyptus and rainforest that tantalized her senses. She breathed in the warm sweet fragrance of his breath as it grazed her cheek. Her stomach muscles clenched.

She quickly moved away from him, reaching out to take Sam's hand. At that precise moment, Sam raced over to Joel placing his hand inside his uncle's. This time the feeling of isolation she experienced was accompanied by another emotion. An alien emotion. Could she possibly be jealous of Sam's affection for Joel? Surely not.

Shaken, she drew away from them.

Cassie spun around at the sound of screeching brakes. A swirl of red dust engulfed her as a land buggy screeched to a halt beside them.

Dust filled her lungs. She coughed while attempting to brush the clinging red dust from her clothes. Impossible. It was hot, dusty, and so damn vast; had she landed on another planet?

A tall, sinewy man with carrot-colored hair unfolded from the front seat. He was in his late forties, his skin tanned to the color of leather by the relentless sun.

His face crinkled into tiny creases as he greeted them. "Hi, Joel," he called. "How woz the trip to Melbourne, successful I hope?"

"More than successful. I discovered I have a family." Joel gently pushed Sam forward. "This is my nephew. Sam, this is Bluey Meadows, my foreman."

Bluey ruffled Sam's hair. "Crikey. How ya goin', mate?"

At Bluey's inquiring glance toward Cassie, Joel said, "And Sam's aunt, Cassie Trenhaile."

Bluey stuck out a large, callused hand. She slipped hers inside his. He shook her hand so vigorously her bones crackled. "Glad to meetcha, Mrs. Trenhaile."

"It's Miss Trenhaile, and please, call me Cassie." She smiled and his grin widened.

"Cassie it'll be then. A welcome to Oriole to you and the young bloke." He spoke to Joel. "I'll get the luggage from the plane."

"Thanks," Joel responded, swinging open the front door of the land buggy.

"Can't we walk to the house?" Cassie asked. Stiff from the cramped position of travelling for hours in the plane, a walk would do them good.

"It's a fair hike. Too far for Sam." Joel glanced down at her high heeled sandals. "And you'll never make it in those. Hope you've brought suitable shoes."

It was the grin that irritated her. That superior, know all smirk that screamed, what would she know about anything. "Of course I've brought suitable shoes," she snapped like a terrier on a bone. "Did you expect me to wear sneakers on the plane?"

He shrugged carelessly. "Hey, as long as you're comfortable."

He knows I'm not comfortable. He knows my legs are burning inside these nylons, but I'll die of heat before I'd confess it to him.

"I feel great."

"Okay." He jerked his thumb in the direction of the land buggy. "Would you rather sit in the front or the back?" He spoke to Sam. "We can squeeze into the back, can't we, Tiger?"

Male buddies, the secret male society that women only dare enter at their own peril. The old he's-my-mate syndrome that she so detested. Was her nephew now a fully-fledged member? "Please don't put yourself out for me." She blew back a hank of hair hanging between her eyes. "The back seat will suit me just fine."

A gentle tug of surprise when he didn't argue. "Right, in you go, then." Joel opened the back door for her. "Before you get sunstroke. And both of you remember, don't go outdoors without hats and sunscreen protection. The heat here can be pretty fierce and with your skin—" He glanced at Cassie, "and especially yours, Cassie, you'll burn like ancient parchment."

Cassie struggled into the back seat. Her knees jammed against the front seat, her hair squashed under the canvas roof of the buggy. "Great," she grumbled. "Just great."

Swinging Sam into front seat of the car, Joel jumped in beside him. He lifted the excited child on to his knee. "Okay, Tiger?"

"Yep."

Bluey loaded their luggage into the back seat beside her. "Sorry about this, Cassie," he apologized and she heard the note of sincerity in his voice and warmed to the rough-and-tumble stockman. "I'd've brought the Land Rover had I known, but I woz only expectin' the boss."

Her shoulders sagged and she couldn't quite manage a grin. When she was sixteen, she'd been shattered when the boy she liked asked her best friend to the school dance. She refused to go at all and no urging from her parents made her change her mind. Like Cinderella sitting by the cinders, she sat alone in her room staring out of the window imagining him kissing her friend. That's how she felt now. Darn, a little self-pity never hurt anyone.

Noisy flocks of thousands of little corellas settling in trees at the side of a watercourse drew her attention. Then the house came into view with its wide cypress veranda wrapped around the front and sides allowing for the spectacular views. Cream-colored weatherboard added subtly to the rustic feel of the home.

The ride was short, and Cassie gladly alighted from the land buggy and followed Joel and Sam toward the house. There was an air of strength and permanency about this house. Distinctive of its owner?

In the garden, green dominated with splashes of vibrant colors in contrast with the home's natural bush setting. A parrot, sweeping in flight, revealed glimpses of rainbow colors.

A woman around fifty, obviously the housekeeper, bustled from the house. She was short and plump, with cropped gray hair, and as she greeted them, a friendly smile lit up her cherry brown eyes. "Welcome home, Joel," she called.

"Berta," he rejoined. "Come and meet Sam and his aunt, Cassie Trenhaile."

Berta held out a hand. "A warm welcome to Oriole, Mrs. Trenhaile."

Cassie sighed, declining to correct the woman on her mistake about her marital status. Instead, she took the older woman's hand and shook it up and down like she was bouncing a rubber ball. She was just so damn nervous. Her scalp itched and her nerves were taut, as if she had been drinking coffee for twenty-four hours straight. "Pleased to meet you, Berta, and please, call me Cassie."

"You must be thirsty and hungry. I've got some freshly brewed coffee and sandwiches made," Berta offered. "They're in the kitchen. Just help yourself any time you want."

"Thanks, I'll appreciate that."

"Did you have a nice trip?"

Cassie glanced over at Joel and they shared a smile. "It was long."

"I don't travel much myself. Happy to stay here on Oriole, I guess." Berta turned to Sam. "And who's this good-looking bloke then?"

"I'm Sam."

"Sam, eh? And have you come to stay with us here on Oriole?"

"Uh-huh. I've come to see my Nana, haven't I, Aunty C?" He kicked dirt with the toe of his sneaker. "And I'll visit you, too, if you want."

Cassie was a little taken aback at the name Sam had chosen for his grandmother. Not once had he heard the name Nana, as they had referred to Joel's mother only as grandmother.

Nana it would be, and she hoped that Mrs. Caine would be equally pleased.

"I reckon I'd like that very much," Berta said, reaching out her hand touched the boy's halo of sandy curls. "You know something, Sam? I feel real excited about your visit."

Sam hopped on one foot, then the other. "Me, too. I'm excited too."

"What's your favorite cake? Is it chocolate or maybe strawberry?"

"Chocolate." His hand circled his tummy. "Yum, yum."

They laughed at Sam's antics and sensing he had the adults full attention, he said, "I love cake the bestest in the world." He sucked in his lower lip and screwed his forehead down in a thoughtful gesture. "Except for McDonald's," he added seriously, and the adults laughed louder.

"Well, seeing it's your best love in the world, and we haven't got a McDonald's for miles and miles, then first thing in the morning I'll make some of my famous lamingtons."

"Lamingtons?" Sam said, as if he hadn't heard the word before.

"You know, Sam," Berta said. "Chocolate-covered sponge cake sprinkled with coconut. Want to help me?"

"Can I lick the icing bowl?"

"What else would I do with the bowl?" She glanced at Cassie. "I'm up early in the mornings. How about you have a lay-in and I'll get the boy up and dressed and ready for the day?"

Fear flashed through Cassie at this wonderful gesture. Would Sam want to stay at Oriole rather than come home with her? A sleep-in sounded tempting. And she was so tired she could sleep a day away. "Are you sure, Berta? He'll drive you crazy with questions."

"I reckon I can handle that."

"Thanks, I'd appreciate it."

Sam yelled with glee as a yellow Labrador, a Springer spaniel and a Blue Heeler rushed to greet them. There were shouts of welcome from men passing the house. The dogs were yelping and jumping around Joel's feet. His housekeeper was chatting to Joel as if he was a long-lost friend. Everyone and everything at Oriole seemed to love Joel, even Sam—no, especially Sam.

Could she be wrong in her judgment of Joel Caine? Could it be that he was a caring, responsible man? He'd offered no explanation and no apology to her on behalf of his brother's treachery to her sister. There was nothing between them but Sam. Sam was Joel's only interest.

Yet she sensed if anyone here were in trouble, Joel would be the person they would go to. She tried to drag her eyes away from his powerful figure, the way he stood with his hands firmly on his hips, legs apart. How familiar his face was to her now as if she'd known him for years. Stupid, really.

Her deepening feelings for Joel startled her. No way could she allow any connection between them except for Sam. That would be too dangerous for her because she couldn't take a chance on him. His brother had played too harshly with women's hearts; made love to them, promised them the world and then crushed them under his boot. Joel had displayed a ruthless streak when he'd threatened her with court proceedings over Sam's custody. She feared that same ruthlessness could be echoed in his treatment of women—just like his brother.

So she'd ignore the fact that he made her breathless. That her heart raced at the sound of his husky voice. That when he'd kissed her she'd been transported to the stars, and she had wanted so much more.

Oh no, she didn't intend to become one of Joel Caine's conquests that he'd earmark with a knife on the side of his saddle.

Sam was rolling in the grass with the dogs, and Cassie's heart sang with joy at the wonderful scene. She knew for sure now that she'd made the right decision in bringing Sam to Oriole. Raised in an apartment, Sam had never experienced the true freedom of having his own space. This was all so wonderful for him.

"What's their names, Uncle Joel?" he cried. Stopping his frolicking he knelt beside the Labrador, his arm loosely wrapped around the big dog's neck.

"This big guy," Joel explained, scratching behind the dog's ear, "is called Jacko. He's pretty old and needs lots of loving. The young spaniel is Ralph, and he needs someone to play with him, and Cracker is an old heeler sheep dog who's too tired to work these days."

"Can I play with Ralph, Uncle Joel? And I can love Jacko and Cracker, too?"

Looking at his nephew, Joel's eyes had softened to a misty blue; strange how much Joel had come to love Sam in such a short time.

"I think you could just about do that, Tiger." He ruffled Sam's hair. "Now off you go with Berta and have a sandwich and a glass of milk."

Cassie's mind whirled as she followed Joel into a sitting room that would rival a ballroom in size. And she was grateful for the rush of cool air. She faced a sprawling area of relaxation and ease. There wasn't much evidence of a woman's touch. Oh, it was spotlessly clean and tidy, too much so, perhaps, and it missed out on things such as vases of fresh flowers scattered around the room, family photographs, a box of knitting or sewing and the joyful mess of a young child. Maybe it was because of his mother's grave illness. What the house looked like she was sure wouldn't be on the top of Mrs. Caine's priority list.

Cassie continued her examination of the room. A crowded bookcase, an eclectic collection of art works, a state-of-the-arts electronic console comprising the latest TV, DVD, and recording facilities, a roll-top desk cluttered with papers and legal-looking documents, and giant-sized furnishings.

There was an almost physical feeling of peacefulness beneath the lofty cathedral ceiling, and the cantilevered timber staircase, which, she imagined, led to the bedrooms above.

Everything reeked of luxury and wealth.

"Joel, it's simply beautiful," she said. "It's like something out of a magazine."

"Thanks." His smile broadened with pride. "It took much time and effort but it was well worth it."

"I wasn't expecting this."

He laughed as if sincerely amused. "Were you expecting a log cabin in the hills?"

She returned his laugh. "Of course not, but I wasn't expecting such luxury."

"Would you like to sit down?" he asked motioning to the armchair.

Gladly, she sank into a soft peach-colored leather armchair. She gave a small sigh. "Now this I could become accustomed to."

With intense eyes and a tiny hint of a smile on his sensual lips, his gaze riveted to her face then moved slowly down over her body. Her heart slammed hard against her chest. *Oh no, here I go again.*

"I want you to be completely at home while you're at Oriole. If you need anything or want anything, just ask Berta or me."

You are not attracted to him, she told herself, but her heart said differently. Her heart told her that he was a man that any woman would want to call her own. Tall, strong, funny, and tender, that's what she had learned about Joel since he'd first knocked on her door.

Oh, add stubborn and determined to have his way—a man in every sense of the word. Never in her life had she met anyone remotely resembling Joel. Sexy, and as hot as bubbling lava—and twice as dangerous. *Stupid heart.* "I can't imagine needing anything more than this." She glanced over at the stairs, anything, and anywhere to avoid his penetrating gaze. "Where's your mother?"

"Upstairs resting, I should imagine. These days she spends more time in her room."

"Does she need full-time care?"

"Berta's a trained nurse."

He hunkered down beside her chair, his face inches from hers. One finger caressed the top of her shoulder. She tried to ignore the strange yearning pulsating deep down inside her. That need, desire that only he could satisfy and an image of them in bed flashed into her mind. Hmm, nice. Her cheeks heated.

Sex, it was all about sex...well, the lack of it. She was sexually attracted to him, and who wouldn't be? Her hormones were dancing a tango, that's all it was.

Please God, let me get out of here still sane, and while you're at it God, an extra heavy dose of self-control so I can resist him.

"We'll go and see her when you and Sam feel more settled."

A worried look crossed his features.

She felt a surge of sympathy for him. He was concerned about his mother and how she may take having Cassie stay. There was the matter of her youngest son's adulterous affair, his untimely death, and now the knowledge that there was a child from the union. How did she truly feel about having a constant reminder of her son's infidelity in her home? Would her welcome be cool but polite?

She glanced at Joel. Did he feel the same way? Did he resent her invasion into his life? What were his true motives bringing her and Sam to Oriole? Did he truly mean it as a short visit or had he more nefarious plans? She worried again that he meant to keep Sam here with him. Fear clutched her belly. How could she fight him here in this vast country? This was his territory and she the intruder.

With an effort she fought back the fear that threatened to take control. Foolish woman. It was, as he'd said, a chance for Sam to get to know his father's family.

As if sensing her discomfort, he stood and moved away from her. "This must be awkward for you?"

"A little."

"I can imagine how strange you must be feeling."

She didn't want his pity and she resented his condescension. This wasn't a holiday for her; she was here to protect Sam; make sure nothing scared or upset him. This would be the first and definitely the last time she'd come to Oriole, and with a bit of restraint, a strong mental attitude, she'd forget Joel Caine ever existed. Suppressing an ironical snort, she acknowledged that forgetting him might well be impossible, but she could sweep him back into the dark regions of her mind and only bring him forth when and if she had to speak to him about Sam.

She relaxed a little. No need for her to be so uptight. She could handle Joel Caine with one hand tied behind her back. After all, he was only a man.

"No more than you and your mother must feel," she said more tightly than intended.

A muscle quivered at his jaw. "What do you mean by that crack?"

She wanted him to talk about the past. She wanted him to admit how wrongly Luke had treated Claudia. She supposed she wanted him to apologize on behalf of his brother. Was that too much to ask? "The guilt you must feel about how your brother treated my sister."

His dark eyes flashed fire. "That's in the past and better forgotten."

Knowing she had to share Sam forever with these people, her trepidation at meeting Joel's mother, and being here in the vast outback and relying on Joel's kindness rushed up to grip her in frustration and bewilderment, which, because she couldn't handle the situation, turned into hostility at Joel's smugness and his refusal to acknowledge his brother's treachery. "How convenient for you. Well, I don't want to forget it," she snapped. "I want to remember how badly your brother treated Claudia and how she suffered from his blatant disregard of her feelings."

"I don't think you want to talk about this, Cassie."

Was that a warning tone in his voice? How dare he bully her? A caveman was more sensitive and had more manners than this outback cowboy.

"Are you so guilty that you refuse to talk about it? Can't you admit what a swine your brother was? You must have known what was going on. Yet you and your mother shut your eyes to the truth. It makes me wonder what sort of woman would teach such low morals to her sons."

He was angry. She could see it in the tug of his mouth, in his eyes, in the tenseness of his body.

He held up one hand. "Don't push this, Cassie."

Her anger responded to his. "Push what? That the Caine family has no principles? That they treat people the way they see fit?"

His fists clenched. "Is that what you think of me?"

"Yes, yes, yes. You have no values, Joel; you were raised thinking the world owes you."

"My brother wanted to be with your sister, but couldn't."

She flattened her palms against the sofa. "Because he was married to another woman."

Talk yourself out of that one. Her statement was righteous; she was, at last, defending her poor misused sister; demanding at least an apology for crimes committed against her.

His jaw thrust forward and his eyes, as blue as the Adriatic Sea, flashed lightning strikes. Battle lines drawn. City girl at odds with outback man.

"Luke believed that Claudia would marry him. He wanted to make his life with her."

"And what did he intend to do with his wife?" Her laugh was mordant. "Or did he envisage a threesome?" Cassie leaned forward. "Luke was married, Joel." Each word hyphenated. "He knew this and yet began an affair with my sister."

"Luke's marriage was over long before he met Claudia." His voice was calm. His gaze was steady.

All the air burst out of her self-righteous balloon. "What?" Her mouth dropped open; she shut it with a clunk.

His mouth twisted wryly. "They'd been divorced for more than a year."

Shock trundled through her. "Are you suggesting—" she swallowed harshly, "Claudia lied to me?"

His expression was a mask of stone. "Yes, she did. I'm sorry."

The weight of the world descended on her. This was so awful. She studied his face and had no cause to doubt him, but resentment, as old as time itself, grated her. She didn't want to believe that Luke was innocent and it was Claudia who'd lied and cheated. Lied to her about Luke being married and cheated him out of the knowledge of his baby.

"He wanted to see her one more time," Joel explained. "And nothing I could say or do would dissuade him." He gave a small cough. "He didn't make it. His plane came down, and he didn't survive."

Tears stung her eyes. "You liar. You damn liar."

She swallowed back the tears. Deep down, where it counted, she knew the truth. Claudia had tired of the affair and dumped him. Then, when she discovered she was pregnant, came to Cassie for help. Knowing that she would insist Claudia tell Luke about the baby, she said he was a married man and refused to leave his wife. Needing to gain Cassie's full sympathy and support, the way Cassie had always done.

She'd never forgive Joel for ruining her memories of her sister. "You know nothing of my sister. You only have your brother's story."

He raked his fingers through his hair. "Why dig up the past. What happened between Luke and Claudia had nothing to do with what's happening now."

"Because I won't have her memory tainted by sordid lies," she cried. She turned away hiding the tears.

The silence between them became unbearable. She turned and faced him. Their eyes met, locked. Winner, loser? A flare of satisfaction blazed as he turned from her, and walked toward a well stocked bar. "Care for a wine?"

She'd die of thirst rather than take a sip of water with Joel Caine. "No thanks."

"Something lighter? A glass of fruit juice, or a mineral water perhaps?"

What hurt the most was that Joel had made her face the truth. Claudia had lied horribly and in so doing had destroyed lives. Cassie remembered her sister's insatiable lust for life. Remembering now the way she'd pout until she got what she wanted. Her ability to twist people around to get her own way. Her beautiful, indulged sister. Her heart ached. All these years she'd harbored hate against a family she didn't know. Blamed the Caines for her sister's heartache and all the time it had been the reverse.

Claudia, oh, Claudia. Tears scalded her throat. She had to get out of this room. Away from Joel. She needed time to think. "I'd like to bathe Sam," she said coming to her feet, "then meet your mother, and put him to bed. He's had a long and very exciting day."

"Of course." He moved away from the bar. "He'll have eaten a light meal now with Berta. Is that enough for him? Will I have Berta make him a more substantial meal?"

She was feeling better now. More in control. "I'm sure that'll do him until morning. Best not to overload him after all that travelling."

"You know best," he conceded.

Sam raced into the room, the dogs close at heel barking and leaping as each one endeavored to get close to the boy. "It seems Sam has won their hearts."

"I think this is only the beginning," he agreed. "He'll have everyone and everything spinning on its axis."

"He's hard to resist." She smiled and held out a hand. "Come on, Sam. Bath time."

Joel moved to join them. "I'll come with you and show you the way."

"Do you think we'll get lost?"

He gave a soft laugh. "Could do."

"This house seems large enough for six families," she said again glancing around the room.

"I need space." He swung the child high on to his shoulder. "I'd like to help bathe him, and then read him a story." He wriggled Sam's legs. "Would you like that, Tiger?"

"Yes," Sam piped.

Cassie followed him upstairs and into a spacious bedroom ideal for a child.

"This is your room, Sam," he said lowering the boy on to the floor. He crouched down before his nephew. "What would you like on the walls?" He swept out his arm. "Spaceships? What about a bed shaped like a star ship?"

Sam clapped his hands in delight. "Maybe we can have big elephants on the walls, Uncle Joel?"

"Elephants sound good."

"Or maybe we can have tigers, lions, and bears," Cassie said.

"Or maybe," Sam giggled, "we could have a zoo with all the animals."

Joel caught on to their game quickly. "And maybe we could have the whole jungle."

"Yes, Uncle Joel," he cried out with delight. "With crocodiles and rhinuses."

Standing erect, his hands on his lean hips, Joel laughed heartily. "All the animals you can think of, Sam and especially rhinuses."

His gaze connected with hers. She smiled and when he grinned back, her heart grew wings and fluttered wildly somewhere in her chest. Oh no, she couldn't allow her feelings for this man to go sky high. She couldn't trust him, wasn't sure about his true intent with Sam. And, if she faced the truth, how could Joel trust her after what her sister did to his brother? What an unholy mess.

Again he looked up at Cassie. She refused to be swamped by the blueness of his eyes, but her resolve ebbed as his gaze slipped over her face like blue velvet.

Sam tugged at her dress. His eyes wide and anxious. "Where will you sleep, Aunty C?"

"I'm not quite sure where—"

Joel interrupted. "Aunty's room is right across the hall and mine's next door to your room."

"If you tell me where the bathroom is?" Cassie said.

He jerked a thumb to a door on the left. "All the bedrooms have their own bathroom."

"You run his bath and I'll undress him," she said, in a tone not unlike a policeman reading your rights. "And don't make the water too hot."

"Yes, ma'am."

"And he likes a lot of bubbles."

"Yes, ma'am," Joel said again with a mock salute and a click of his heels, and Sam broke into a fit of giggles.

Cassie gave them both a disdainful glare as she knelt down and undressed her nephew.

Never had bath time been so much fun. There were soap bubbles on every conceivable surface. "If you have any more bubbles, Sam, we won't be able to find you."

"Bubbles tickle your nose, don't they, Uncle Joel?"

Joel scooped up a handful of bubbles and smeared them thickly across his upper lip. "How do I look with a moustache, Sam?"

"Funny." Sam giggled.

An hour later, when Sam was snug in his dressing gown and slippers, and Cassie had showered and changed, Joel took them to meet his mother.

Outside his mother's bedroom, Joel looked down at Cassie. "Okay?"

Cassie swallowed back the knot forming in her throat. She'd been nervous enough before when she believed Luke had been the wrongdoer. Whatever did this woman think of her, knowing what her sister had done to her younger son? "As I can be."

He squeezed her hand, and she appreciated the comfort and warmth it gave her. "Everything will be fine. Don't worry." He gave a small rap on the door and they entered the room.

Queenie Caine sat in a king-size four-poster bed supported by mounds of white lace pillows. Her eyes were closed.

A glance at the bedside table revealed several bottles of medication and a respirator. On all counts it appeared that Queenie Caine was indeed a very sick woman. The glance also revealed a handsome face laughing out from a photograph held inside an antique silver frame. Cassie took an educated guess that this was Joel's brother. From the corner of the frame dangled an open silver locket, which revealed a tuft of golden hair.

It has to be Luke's baby hair. Dear God...

Further to the right of the table was a nest of photographs—all of her youngest son from the time he was born until his untimely death.

Cassie closed her eyes as a wave of giddiness overtook her. Whatever would this woman say to her, and what could she say to Queenie Caine? *Hey, so my sister messed up. Them's the breaks.* The situation was impossible.

Sam was all these people wanted. He was their pride and joy, their hope for the future of Oriole. Cassie was a by-product. Someone they should be nice to, to make it so much easier to get rid of without fuss. *Don't call us, we'll call you.*

Queenie's eyes fluttered open. "Joel," she murmured.

The love he held for his mother rushed up into two little words. "Hi, love. I've brought someone to meet you."

Gathering her remnants of confidence, Cassie took Sam by the hand and approached the bedside. "Mrs. Caine," she chose her words carefully, "this is your grandson, Sam." She pushed Sam slightly in front of her. "Sam, please say hello to your grandmother."

Sam approached the bed staring curiously at his grandmother. "Are you sick?"

Smiling, Queenie reached out and touched his face. "A little," she confessed.

"I was sick last time. I had a bad, bad tummy ache, but it's gone now." He spread his arms wide open. "I was this sick."

Queenie laughed. "I don't think I'm going to be so sick now that you've come to stay with me."

"I've come for a visit." He looked up at his aunt for encouragement.

Cassie nodded and tried to smile reassuringly.

"And I'm so glad you have." Still holding Sam's hand, Queenie looked up at Cassie. "I'm Queenie." She held out a slender white hand.

Cassie took Queenie's hand firmly in her own and a feeling of warmth engulfed her. She knew instinctively that she would like Queenie Caine. That Joel's mother wasn't at all like she'd imagined her to be. Not that she was sure what she had expected, but certainly not this graciously warm and good-natured woman now holding her hand.

"I'm Cassie," she whispered, "Sam's Aunty C," simply because she didn't know what else to say.

Queenie's delicate beauty astounded her. Her hair, the color of honeycomb, was swept into a thick coil at the base of her neck. Her skin was so translucent you could see the crisscrossing tiny blue rivers of veins.

Although purged by her sickness, Queenie was a hauntingly beautiful woman. She smiled and the warmth of that smile glow through Cassie.

"Welcome to Oriole, Cassie. Thanks for bringing Sam." She touched Sam's hair. "I can't begin to tell you how wonderful it is to have a grandson. Luke's son."

Turning away from them, Queenie coughed gently into a white lace handkerchief. "Would you like to come and see me tomorrow, Sam?"

He nodded. "And, Nana, I'll read you my bestest ever story book."

"That would be grand," Queenie whispered slumping back against the pillow.

Placing her hand on top of Sam's shoulder, Cassie said, "It's time to go to your room and choose a book for me to read to you."

The boy moved reluctantly toward the open bedroom door. He swung on the doorknob. "Will you come to my room and read me the story, too, Uncle Joel?"

"Try and stop me, Tiger."

"Goodnight, Nana," Sam called as he skipped out of the room and down the hall to his own.

Queenie gave a wracking cough.

Joel moved to her side concern flooding his face. "You're tired," he said softly. "This has been far too much strain on you."

Queenie laughed. "Don't fuss so, darling. I'm perfectly all right." She sighed. "But you're right, I am tired." She looked at Cassie. "Thank you again, Cassie for bringing my grandson to me."

"My pleasure, Mrs. Caine."

"And Cassie, do you think—no, I know you and I can be friends."

"Oh, Mrs. Caine, so do I."

She reached out and touched Cassie's hand. "Then, my dear, let's begin our friendship by you calling me Queenie."

Joel, bending over, kissed his mother's cheek. He brushed her hair gently back from her forehead. "Rest now, love, and we'll see you in the morning."

Cassie preceded Joel from the bedroom. She waited while he closed the bedroom door. He faced her, and the look on his face worried her.

"Aunty C," Sam called, "Uncle."

"Coming," they said in unison and laughed together.

She glanced at Joel's profile as he read Sam a bedtime story from his favorite book. Such a handsome man, a man any woman would be proud to call her own. A deep stirring in her heart. She desired Joel with a need that was deep. She understood and accepted this, but she also accepted that that's as far as it went. She'd never cross the line with him. She wanted to leave Oriole the same way she came, sane and unbroken.

"He's asleep," Joel said.

Cassie bent over the sleeping child and kissed his flushed cheek, brushing the curls back from his forehead. "He's exhausted."

"He's had a big day."

"He'll settle in and get into a routine in no time," she reassured him.

Joel towered over her and she moved a few steps back from his overpowering presence. "Sorry, if I overstep the boundaries with Sam. I'm not used to being Uncle Joel yet."

Again, he'd surprised her with his unexpected candor. "I can get a bit possessive at times. I have to learn to share him more."

He moved in, she moved back. "That's understandable; you've had him on your own for so long it must be difficult for you."

"Yes, it's difficult but not impossible," she conceded. "Sam needs you and your mother in his life."

His smile was like a bolt of lightning and had the same effect. "Have you any family, Cassie?"

"I have no one but Sam."

"I'm sorry to hear that." His voice dropped in volume. "It must have been tough for you—you know—when you were left on your own with a small baby."

It pleased her that he at least showed concern for what had happened. "I coped."

As they moved out of Sam's room and into the hall, he said, "I've a few things to attend to that shouldn't take too long. You'll join me for dinner, won't you?" His gaze caressed her features.

"I'm very tired, Joel. I'd prefer to have a light meal in my room."

"Eating alone gives you indigestion."

"I'll risk it."

"Aw, come on, Cassie, relax a little. Would it hurt you too much to eat with me? Besides I'm tired of eating alone."

He sounded so like Sam when he wanted his own way that she couldn't help relenting. "Okay."

Reaching over, he entwined his fingers through her hair and gently moved her head toward him, brushing her lips with his. It was only a fleeting kiss, but it was enough to make the blood pulsate wildly through her veins. She fell back against the wall, touching her lips with the tips of her fingers. "Don't kiss me." He touched her cheek with his fingertips. Her head jerked back and banged against the wall. "Ouch."

"We have to be friends. We'll be seeing each other every day."

Could he keep it at just friends? Could she? Sex with this cowboy would be good. "Friends do not keep kissing each other on the mouth."

"Yeah?" He cocked his head. "Why not?"

"They just don't."

"I was trying to express my feelings," he said smoothly, his face expressionless. "Sam being here. How happy it's made my mother. The way you said you'd be friends with her."

She was totally aware of his sexiness, his seemingly innate ability to see inside her, his ability to be empathetic and understanding.

Before she could answer, he said, "I'll see you downstairs in the dining room in say," he glanced at his watch, "half an hour."

Her head ached slightly. Her skin prickled. She didn't want to eat a meal with him—she didn't want to share a packet of peanuts with him.

She sighed as he took the stairs two at a time.

Moving into the room, she sat on the edge of the enormous bed and without warning the room seemed so empty and so strange that she was lost. She fought the urge to run to Sam's room and climb into bed with him. Feel the warmth of his tiny body against hers. Breathe in his sweet just washed little boy smell.

She fell back on the bed her arms outstretched above her head and stared at the delicately carved ceiling.

"Great," she muttered. "Just great."

She'd promised to have dinner with a man who had her insides turning like she was sailing on rough seas. If it weren't for Sam's claim to the Caine dynasty and the right to know his family, she'd be running from here as fast as her legs would allow. But for now she was stuck here with Joel and he was far too dangerous for her sanity. The sooner their sojourn was over, the better.

CHAPTER NINE

Cassie showered and changed into a strapless dress of lemon print cotton and low-heel jade sandals. Not too much make-up, applying only the faintest touch of eye shadow and mascara to her eyes and a smear of pale pink gloss to her lips.

Satisfied with her appearance, and with one last fluff of her hair she descended the stairs.

As soon as she entered the room, Joel rose from his chair and strode fluidly towards her.

He had changed into fresh designer jeans, the striking deep blue of his shirt enhancing his eyes. Joel hadn't gelled his hair, and a lock had fallen across his forehead, the rest thick and wild around the collar of his shirt.

Totally masculine, devilishly handsome, and at ease in his surroundings, she was a fool to imagine that something more than Sam could ever connect them.

Hell, she didn't want a gold band and she didn't want promises; what she needed from Joel he could give her now. She was acutely conscious of his heartthrob magnetism. His vitality. His power. His broad and muscular chest. "I checked on Sam; he's fast asleep," Cassie said.

"It can't be easy. I mean, with you having to work—being a single parent," Joel said.

"My parents left me money. That's how I started my photography business."

"Going well?"

"I make a decent living. I freelance, and my publisher wants me to do an outback spread. Is that okay with you if I take photographs here?"

"Sure. Anything you need?"

"I've brought my equipment."

Reaching out, he took her hand inside his. He rubbed his thumb across her knuckles, over the soft skin under her wrist. With a small almost apologetic smile, she withdrew her hand from his, and tried to ignore the tingle of excitement that coursed up her arm.

She moved her mouth close to his. Their breaths mingled. She was aroused in every way possible. Her breathing labored as her heart went into fast forward. She pressed her mouth fully over his.

Clasping the back of his head, she drew him down and kissed him again, thrusting her tongue deep inside his mouth. Waves of desire plunged through her. "You really must try to stop kissing me, Joel."

"I thought you were kissing me."

"Now would I take advantage of a situation?"

"Yeah, I think you would."

"Kissing from now on is out."

"It's difficult for me." He grinned. "What can I do about it?"

"I don't know, maybe if you chewed gum?" She laughed softly. "I don't want you to become a habit."

"Aw, I'm a creature of habit."

She sat on the oversized avocado-colored sofa, and he said, "I'm having a drink. Would you like one?"

"Lemonade would be nice."

He poured her drink, handed her the glass, and sat in a chair opposite her.

While sipping her lemonade, Cassie looked around the room with great interest. There was a large painting of Sydney over the mantelpiece. She could see the graceful sails of the Opera House and the sharp clean lines of their famous Harbour Bridge. She glanced up at the large, yet delicate, crystal chandelier hanging gracefully from the ornate ceiling. This was truly a beautiful house.

"What do you think of Oriole so far?"

"I knew your station would be large, but I never imagined anything as big as this."

He smiled with obvious pride. "Most are surprised when they come here. Do you ride?"

"Yes, but only city riding. You know, horse trails, that sort of thing."

"We'll go riding one day and I'll show you Oriole at its best."

"Sounds great."

"And while we're on the subject, don't go riding on your own. Okay, Cassie?"

"Why not?"

"You could get lost. In fact, you most probably would get lost. Turn around twice out in the bush and you're disorientated."

She shrugged. "I wouldn't venture too far."

"I said don't go riding, not without me or one of the men." He frowned. "Okay, Cassie?"

"Okay," she muttered. Worrywart. She liked horse riding very much and went as often as she could. Sam was learning to ride, even at his young age, and loved it. She could handle a short ride around the station. She glanced at him. He was still frowning. Still, best not to upset Joel any more than she had to. Subject change time. "Do you breed only cattle?"

He sipped his ice-cold beer. "We have a few pigs and chickens for domestic use."

"And how do you get anything else you need?"

"Flown in from Derby."

"What if Sam gets sick or hurts himself?" She voiced her concerns.

His gaze came to rest on her questioning eyes. "As I told you, Berta's a trained nurse."

"What if he's seriously hurt?"

"I can fly him to Derby Hospital. If he can't be moved, I'd call in the flying doctor and he can be treated here and then taken to hospital. Anything else worrying you?"

"Everything sounds great."

"Care for another lemonade?"

"No, thanks."

"Berta has prepared a light meal. Are you hungry?" he asked, pointing to a table in the far corner of the room she had not previously noticed. It was laden with a deliciously tempting cold collation.

Her stomach growled. "Famished."

He followed her to the table where they selected chicken, ham, and delicious-looking salads from the dishes laid out.

While he chose a breast of chicken, she studied his profile. The strong chin, the slightly crooked nose, that ever-straying lock of blond hair.

"You must try some of Berta's potato salad. It's to die for."

Totally unprepared for him to speak, her hand jerked and food toppled from her plate, and slices of tomato soaked into the stark white tablecloth. "Oh, no," she muttered, dabbing at the offending food with a paper napkin.

"Hey, Cassie, don't worry. I mess up all the time."

Cheeks flaming, she returned to the sofa and ate with a daintiness that would shame a heroine out of a Victorian novel.

Joel ate his meal, never removing his ever-alert gaze until she finished eating. He then approached her. "Finished?"

She nodded.

"Can I tempt you with more?"

"Er, no. I've had elegant sufficiency."

He took the now empty plate and placed it on the table. "Care for some music?"

"Nice."

"Any preferences?"

"Nothing too heavy."

"Edith Piaf?"

"Lovely." She rested her head back against the sofa as the sounds of *Non, Je Ne Regrette Rien* filled the room. The music brought to mind Piaf's sad life and the way the title and lyric so eloquently expressed her attitude to life. In her private life, Piaf was as tormented as the heroines of her songs, and she'd had many relationships, most causing her severe emotional damage.

It made Cassie wonder at the frailties of women where the men they loved were concerned.

She stirred restlessly as Joel left his chair and sat on the sofa next to her. He placed his arm across the back of sofa, behind her head, his fingers idly playing with the loose strands of her hair. She fought the urge to jump his bones. Instead she said, "It's been a long day and I'm bushed. I'll say good night and hit the sack."

He scrambled to his feet. "I'm so unaccustomed to having guests at Oriole it seems I've forgotten my manners."

He took her hand and she pretended she didn't care, pretended that the touch of his hand on hers wasn't sweet and comforting.

Fool.

What if she fell in love with him? Where would that leave her? Up a muddy creek with no paddle.

Loving Joel would hurt.

Besides, she had no intention of falling for him. He was handsome and sexy and her hormones were raging—quite natural, really. Just a case of "your bed or mine."

Too much water under the bridge. His brother's life was ruined through Claudia's lies and false recriminations and her own difficulty in accepting and admitting the truth. Then there was the ugly question of whether or not Joel wanted to keep Sam on Oriole. Cassie's heart ached.

He'd be glad if she left Sam here on Oriole and then disappeared from Joel's life as if she'd never existed.

She would never be convinced otherwise.

...

This red-headed woman had him jumping. Her green eyes, the way she moved and talked, her love for Sam, and her defense of her sister showed him what a proud and in control woman she was. He found it difficult to keep his hands in his pockets. Why did she occupy his thoughts dawn to dusk? The taste of her mouth. Okay, so he wanted her. Surely that was normal. She was a beautiful, sexy woman any man would want in his bed.

He ran his hands over his face. Idiot. He didn't want to start anything with Cassie that couldn't be finished. Too much at stake here. Sam was important to him, his grandmother, and for the future of Oriole.

He had no intention of letting Sam go now that he was here on Oriole. And he knew Cassie would fight tooth and nail to keep him.

He closed his eyes and concentrated on his problem. There had to be a way.

What he had to work out was how not to hurt Cassie.

CHAPTER TEN

After a restless night, Cassie woke feeling leaden and lethargic. She had tossed and turned for hours, finally falling into a drug-like sleep.

She looked around the beautiful room she'd slept in. Any woman would love to live in such a grand house.

Melbourne seemed a long way away. Another world, another time, and another life. A life without Joel.

She crawled out of bed, wrapping a white terrycloth bathrobe around her body.

Cassie moved to the open window and took a whiff of the soft warm air. She stared into the vastness that was Oriole. Over five hundred thousand acres of magnificent outback country stretched before her. Untouched by nature, everything was how it was meant to be. And most of its inhabitants were the cattle that roamed and dined on its rich, green pastures.

She'd studied the map of Australia that lined the large wall of the library. The Kimberley wasn't too difficult to locate, situated at the far north of Western Australia.

Then a book on the Kimberley caught her attention. When she had returned to her room, she spent ages reading up on the area. From the Pearl Coast of Broome in the west to the historic town of Wyndham in the east, the Kimberley was a vast and exciting wilderness area. It was one of the most remote regions of Australia and was considered one of its last wilderness frontiers.

Shouts of laughter made her look down. Sam was in the garden with Berta. Cassie raised the window higher and leaned out, "Hi, down there. What's going on?"

Sam waved. "Hi, Aunty C," he yelled. "Berta got me out of bed and dressed me, and I came down with her to the kitchen, and we had breakfast and I ate it all up. Didn't I, Berta?"

"You sure did, Sam. You ate every last crumb."

"Good boy, Sam. What are you doing now?"

Of course Sam would think it so wonderful being on Oriole, and having Berta's kindness, Joel taking him under his wing, protecting him, guiding him, and his grandmother to love him. She felt a sense of sadness; this was all a little boy could wish for.

"I'm playing with Berta." He grabbed a ball and tossed it into the air, catching it on its downward journey. "See how good I are? I catched the ball."

"Very clever, Sam." She smiled at the housekeeper. "Morning, Berta."

"Good-morning, Cassie. It's a wonderful day."

"Seems too hot already."

"Hot? Are you kidding? This is mild."

Cassie laughed. "I'm used to Victoria and its four seasons in a day weather."

"You'll love it here—when you get used to the heat, that is."

"Have you been here long?"

"Born and bred in Derby. I came to Oriole a few years back when my husband died, and my kids had all grown up and travelled away. Joel advertised for a companion for his mother, so I came here to look after the missus while she's crook. Sort of fell into looking after Joel as well."

"I imagine they can't do without you now."

"Don't reckon they can." Berta shielded her eyes against the glare of the sun. "I'll prepare you some breakfast when you come down."

Food did nothing to excite her. "Don't bother. Although I'd like some coffee, if that's not too much trouble."

"Trouble? No trouble at all. I'll leave coffee on the veranda. Just help yourself when you're ready. Is it all right if Sam stays with me? He's going to help me make those lamingtons."

"Thanks, I'd appreciate that."

Showered and dressed in a loose flowing skirt of Indian cotton and matching shirt, Cassie made her way to the veranda. It was only nine o'clock and sticky hot already. Outside on the gravel path, the old Labrador lay on his side, panting as if he hadn't had a drink of water for days. The bees didn't buzz around the flowers with their usual high spirits. They seemed content to stay on the one bud and then fly listlessly off into the sky.

There was a promise in the air of days of endless heat. She glanced at the sky. It was cloudless and an austere blue.

Everything was in readiness for her on the verandah. Berta was a veritable gem. With a flick of the switch, the percolator dripped black aromatic coffee into the glass jug.

She poured coffee into a cup and with a what-the-heck shrug to her shoulders, stirred in a dollop of cream and one sugar. She tasted the coffee. "I need the boost," she said aloud, and added another spoonful of sugar.

Cup in hand, she sat back in a chair, crossed her legs, sipped her coffee, and thought of the only thing that had occupied her mind since he had walked into her life—Joel.

Outside the mesh wire enclosure she heard the soft bell-like notes of the black-banded whiteface. And a sense of wellbeing overcame her.

In the distance, Joel approached the house. Her heart took up a familiar stirring. He strode like a man with purpose, as if he owned the universe and felt right about its possession. As if he knew what he was about and lived his life the way he chose, afraid of nothing, allowing nothing to stand in his way towards achieving his goal.

He'd created Oriole from bare, harsh ochre land—worked hard and long to make the station the success it was. Now he was wealthy and could rest on his laurels, but that wasn't what he was made of. He took life by the horns and grappled it into submission.

He was a few feet away now. He removed his hat and wiped the sweat from his brow with the back of his hand. The sun glinted on his hair like fire on gold. And, as if he knew she was staring at him, his lean hips swaggered.

His raw energy. His blatant sexuality. The sheer height and breadth of him took her breath away.

There were not many men who commanded attention completely as Joel did. When he walked into a room all eyes fixed on him. The air crackled around him. He gave off an aura of strength, instilled a confidence that somehow he would make everything right and just knowing him made a person feel secure.

"Coffee smells good."

So deep in thought, she jerked, and coffee spilt on to her skirt. "Help yourself," she said, dabbing at the stain with a napkin.

His laugh was friendly. "You always seem to be spilling your food."

She smiled. "I need a keeper."

His blue eyes twinkled. "Hmm, I'm a pretty good watchdog. Want I should watch over you?"

"Don't bother, I'll wear a bib."

"Where's Sam?"

"In the kitchen with Berta. She's taken quite a shine to him and evidently the reverse applies." She hesitated then said, "This is great for him here at Oriole."

His smile broadened. "This is Sam's home, now and in the future."

Dread washed through her and a warning bell sounded at the back of her head. It wasn't what he said, it was how he said it. As if Sam would never leave here.

Leaning back, he hooked his thumbs inside the waistband of his jeans. Their eyes connected. His gaze lazily appraised her. "Yours, too, if you want." His voice had an infinitely compassionate tone. He was assuming she would have to return to Melbourne without Sam. No way would she do that; Melbourne was her life, she loved it, couldn't wait to get back to it. But Sam was coming with her. She'd happily let him stay with the Caines in school holidays, anything more than that was definitely a no-go.

"Thanks."

"Are you feeling at home here? No problems? Everything okay?"

"Everything's fine."

"If you need anything, you'll let me know?"

"Yes, of course.

As he poured his coffee, she couldn't take her gaze away from him. His blond hair, ruffled by the wind, tumbled gently down his forehead, and the glorious blue of his eyes outshone the vivid blue of the sky behind him.

He lowered into a chair opposite her. Placing the heels of his boots on to another chair, he crossed his long, well-muscled legs, uttering a small sigh of satisfaction.

There was so much more to this man than just male beauty. There was intelligence, honor, and a fierce pride, and something else, something so vital it took her breath away - tenderness.

"You must have been up early this morning."

"New cattle arrived," he said placing his cup on to the table. "Any biscuits?"

"Yes." She pushed a plate of homemade ginger nuts within his reach.

He chose the largest on the plate, and took a generous bite. "I want to take Sam on a camping trip. Show him some of Oriole, and the outlying areas. Give him a feel of the place." He finished off the biscuit.

Camping in such rough terrain? She frowned, her chest tightening. "He's too young," she protested.

"Old enough to begin learning about his inheritance," he assured her.

"I don't know. He's only four."

He gazed deeply into her eyes. "But he'll be with me. I wouldn't let anything hurt Sam. Ever."

"How long will you be gone?"

"Not long. A couple of days—three at the most." He added, with a grin that immediately reminded her of Sam when he was about to do something mischievous, "Aw, but Cassie, you must come, too."

Her eyes flew wide open. "Me! I'd spoil your trip."

His grin was wicked. Her heart beat a tattoo. "I doubt that. Would you like to come?"

Desert storms? Black nights full of blue stars? Alone with Joel? Hmm, nice image. "Yes, very much, except—"

"Except what?"

"I have this innate fear of snakes. Ridiculous I suppose." She shrugged.

"I can't say, there are no snakes in the outback so it's rare that you're bothered by them."

She weighed him with a critical squint. "Do you have a tent with a wood plank floor and a zip up front?"

"Swag."

"Swag?" she repeated. "I've never quite known what that is, exactly."

"It's a bush-traveler's bundle, a portable canvas bed or sleeping bag for outback travel."

"Sounds deluxe. Every woman should have one."

He winked. "Comes in a variety of colors," he teased.

She grinned. "I must tell you I failed miserably as a camper. When I was a kid, my nanny insisted we go; she said camping was a way of conversing with nature."

"You went camping with your grandmother?"

"No, my nanny. My parents travelled a lot. I had a nanny until I was ten, then I went to boarding school."

He raised a bushy eyebrow. "Surely that's unusual?"

"My parents were unusual."

"How old were you when they died?"

"I was seventeen. Claudia was thirteen."

He shot up. "My God, then you raised Claudia as well."

"Seems I was meant to have children, but something went wrong somewhere."

Joel's eyebrows rose, encouraging her to go on with her story.

"After many attempts, Nanny finally got a fire going. She asked me to pour some water from her five-liter carrier into a ridiculously small tin-billy to boil for tea. She got out bacon and sausages to cook over the flames." She breathed out on a long sigh.

"What happened?"

"I tripped and upended the water. I doused the fire, ruined her only box of matches, and swamped the bacon and sausages." She ignored his laughter and continued. "Nanny took me home swearing it was her last camping adventure with me." She cocked her head. "Still want me to go?"

He wiped his eyes with the back of his hand. "I'll keep you away from the fire. My dad had me out in the bush as soon as I took my first step."

"I suppose you were branding cattle, breaking-in wild brumbies, and leaping tall buildings in a single bound at five?"

"Something like that."

His feet came to the floor as he leaned toward her. He was so handsome that her blood soared through her veins like a thunderous waterfall. She concentrated on a red-winged parrot feeding on the seeds of eucalypts. The beautiful bird raised its wings for a moment before flying away with deliberate, rhythmic wingbeats, weaving its way through the trees with remarkable dexterity.

He leaned over and kissed the tip of her nose. "I'm taking Sam with me now."

"Where?"

"The yards. Meet the men. Show him the animals. He'll love that."

He was right. Sam would enjoy it all. Love every second of it.

He stood, and raising her from the chair, took her in to his arms. "We won't be long."

"I'll go talk to Queenie."

She knew he was going to kiss her. Oh no, not again. Never again. "Don't even think about it, Joel," Cassie warned.

He laughed. "What?"

"And don't act the innocent. You were going to kiss me."

"Maybe, maybe not." He leant in and wound his arm around her waist. Her heart fluttered as excitement caught her unawares. "You smell so good," he murmured lowering his head his mouth touched hers.

She moved away from him. "No means no, Joel."

"Sorry. I overstepped the mark. Won't happen again."

"So you keep telling me."

With a nod he left her. Cassie felt very alone.

CHAPTER ELEVEN

Cassie spent time in the library reading. Around eleven, and in search of company, she left the library, climbed the stairs and knocked on Queenie's door. At her response, Cassie entered the bedroom, and was acknowledged by a welcoming smile.

"Good morning, Cassie." Queenie put down the book she was reading, and took off her glasses. "What a pleasant surprise. I was hoping you'd come and visit me."

"I wondered if I could get you something to drink or eat? Tea or coffee, a slice of cake, maybe? Berta's baked a batch of lamingtons."

"Talking to you is enough." She patted the edge of the bed. "Sit beside me."

Cassie nestled on to the edge of the bed. Queenie looked so much better today; there was a flush in her cheeks that hadn't been there yesterday, and her eyes were bright. Seeing her grandson had definitely cheered her up no end. Just what the doctor ordered.

"I can't tell you how much it means to have my grandson at Oriole. It's been too long since I've heard the sound of a child laughing and playing."

"He's settling in well."

Queenie covered the top of Cassie's hand with her own. "You've done such a wonderful job raising Sam. He's a delightful child, intelligent, naturally inquisitive, and loving. I could tell that instinctively the first moment I met him."

"He's never been any different."

"You must be proud of him."

Pride filled her heart. If she'd had Sam made to order he couldn't have been more perfect. "Yes. I am, very much so."

Queenie glanced over at the portraits on the table beside her bed. It was Luke about the same age as Sam. The similarities were striking.

"If only we'd known sooner about Luke's son, we could have helped you more." She gave a small rasping cough. "You had so much to bear—the death of your sister. Being left alone with a tiny baby."

"It's okay. I managed."

"I know how difficult this must be for you, Cassie. Here with us."

"It's all right." Cassie's throat closed. "Truly, I don't mind. And it can't be easy for you either. Having me here as a constant reminder of what happened between your son and my sister."

"But it gave us Sam, didn't it?"

"Yes," Cassie whispered. "It gave us Sam."

"Is Joel treating you well? He's not used to company, I'm afraid, and has become somewhat of a loner."

"He's been very kind to me. Making me feel truly at home here at Oriole. You, too, Queenie. Thanks for that." She lowered her eyes and played with the lace cloth on Queenie's bedside table. "Do you have many visitors?"

"Not enough. I'm used to the solitude—in fact, I appreciate it."

Boldly, Cassie asked, "Why did he—why did Joel never marry?"

"So he hasn't told you anything?"

Cassie shook her head.

"Many years ago he loved a girl very much. They married."

Something indescribable surged through Cassie's veins. "Joel's married?"

Queenie wet her lips with the tip of her tongue. "Pour me a glass of water, please, Cassie."

With trembling hand, Cassie passed her the tumbler of water, waited while Queenie had her fill, took the empty glass from her, and placed it back on the bedside table.

"Gabriel, Joel's father, owned a small property in New South Wales. One winter, he fell from his horse and broke his neck." Queenie's voice thickened. "After that Joel became restless, and I knew he wouldn't stay much longer on his father's station. Too many memories for him to cope with." She reached for the white lace handkerchief tucked inside her sleeve, and wiped her eyes.

"He loved his father very much, you see. So we sold the station and moved to Sydney. After awhile Joel left for Africa and got a job with one of the diamond mines. Within a few years, he was a partner. He eventually sold his interest in Africa and came back to Australia and created Oriole."

Queenie sighed. "On a visit to Sydney he met Madeleine Phillips."

Unable to hold back the questions, Cassie asked, "What happened to her? Where is Joel's wife now? Why isn't she here with him?"

"Madeleine was told she'd never have a baby. Yet within six months of their marriage, she fell pregnant. I'd never seen Joel so happy. They counted the months until the birth of their baby." Her expression was one of wretchedness. "Madeleine died giving birth to a boy. My grandson lived for only a few minutes and then joined his mother. That was five years ago now. Joel blames himself and carries the heavy burden of guilt with him. Nothing I say or do makes things right for him."

Cassie felt a gush of sympathy for Joel. Losing his wife and baby son would be too much for any man to endure, and then his brother not much later. "Oh, poor Joel."

"It was an awful time for him. He was inconsolable."

"It must have taken him a long time to get over Madeleine and his son." She sought and found Queenie's eyes. "If he ever did."

"For a long time, I never thought I'd see him smile again, but time has a way of easing and eventually Joel came back to me."

"You think he's healed?"

"I think he's accepted. I doubt he'll ever really heal."

Cassie pondered on that well after she'd left Queenie's room.

CHAPTER TWELVE

Later that same day, a drover was seriously hurt and Joel had left hours ago to be with the injured man.

Cassie had fed and bathed Sam, spent an hour with Queenie, and, leaving Sam with his grandmother, was now downstairs waiting for Joel.

Like a wife waits for her husband?

Like an impatient woman waits for her lover?

Joel telephoned around seven. "Hi," he said, and her toes curled in her sandals.

"How's Jim?"

"We're at the Derby Hospital. I want to stay until I'm satisfied he's okay."

"Are you all right?"

"Yeah, tired but I'm fine. How about you? Are you okay?"

Warmth at his concern filled her. "Yes, of course."

"Sam in bed?"

"He's with your mother. She's reading him his third story."

"They're becoming inseparable."

"He loves her," she said with hesitation, "and you."

"Do you really think so?"

"He talks about you all the time. What you do. What you say. He wants to be like you, Joel."

"I like that thought."

"Then hold on to it, because it's true."

"He's so very special."

"He's been asking after you. I told him where you were and why. He made me promise that you'd kiss him good night when you got home."

"I won't forget."

Cassie heard hospital sounds in the background—the urgent intercom call for a doctor, the soft murmur of voices. She could almost smell the antiseptic, and her fear for Jim Browne grew. She hoped Jim would be all right. Queenie had told her that he had a wife and four kids to look after. He was needed and loved. Cassie closed her eyes and sent up a silent prayer for the injured man.

"Have to go. Will you wait up for me?"

Against her better judgment, she said, "Yes."

"See you soon."

"Goodbye, Joel," she said and clunked the receiver on to the hook.

Cassie walked forlornly around the room, touching an ornament here, moving a chair, running her fingers along the smoothness of the dark wood of a table, feeling the softness of a silk cushion.

She drank in the fresh odor of polishing wax and the heady smell of irises and daffodils she'd placed in a tall crystal vase that stood in the middle of the dining room table.

Walking to the window and drawing back the lace curtain, she stared out at the gathering dusk.

A small group of pink cockatoos, in the company of little corellas and the aerial acrobatics of pink and white galahs, moved toward their roosting trees. The cockatoos raised their crests for a moment after alighting.

Leaving her post by the window and walking from the room, Cassie went upstairs.

She said goodnight to Queenie and tucked Sam into his bed.

After indulging in a hot scented bath, she chose to wear a white lace top and a white silk circle skirt. The pale yellow ankle-strap sandals she wore were barely more than crisscrossing straps.

She styled her hair with attitude, twisting curly bunches of her hair into knots at the back of her head.

She applied her make-up—moist skin and barely beige eyes were pumped up with rosy cheeks and natural crushed cranberry stained lips. A dash of Gucci Envy and she was ready to face the world—well, Joel anyway.

She peeped in Sam's room; he was sleeping peacefully. How much he loved being here at Oriole with Joel and his grandmother, and how important these people had become to him in such a short time, as Sam had to them, Cassie knew.

She walked softly over the lush blue carpet and stared down at the sleeping child.

I want the best for you, Sam. I only want you to know love and happiness for as long as you can.

She leaned down and kissed his warm cheek. He murmured in his sleep.

Sleep tight, my little love. I love you more than I could ever say.

She moved downstairs and entered the library. Earlier she had spread a white linen supper cloth, delicately embroidered with tiny pink roses and sprigs of pale green fern, over a small coffee table in the far corner of the room.

She'd imagined Joel would be tired and hungry when he got home. As Berta was sitting with the injured man's wife, Cassie had prepared Joel sandwiches, adding tiny strawberry tarts to the plate that Berta had prepared earlier that day, covering them in film wrap to keep them fresh. She had promised Berta that she would look after things here, and she would.

She glanced at the clock. Ten-thirty. Maybe he'd decided to stay overnight in Derby. She swallowed down her disappointment.

She chose a CD, Jason Mraz and his band, and placed it into the CD player. Chills crept up her spine but not in an unpleasant way. He was there.

Her gaze flew to the door. He was standing there looking at her, and how long he'd been there was impossible to say. His expression was a riddle to her, yet it made her heart beat frantically and desire flooded her like a morning deluge of summer rain.

She couldn't work him out, this man from the outback. Didn't know what he was thinking. What he was feeling. All she knew was that he turned her upside-down and made her feel as inept as a teenager at her first dance.

A knot formed in her throat as he crossed the room. Cassie resisted the temptation to fall into his arms and cover his mouth with her own.

"You look somewhat presentable."

"Don't overdo the compliments. I may grow to like them." She drew in a deep breath. "Is Jim all right?"

Apprehensive, she touched her hair. Was it all right? Was she overdressed? Was her make-up too heavy? Too light?

She'd wanted so much to look lovely for this man but was doubtful she had succeeded. She gazed deep into his eyes, and all her doubts disappeared under the thrilling comprehension that this man wanted her.

"He's okay. A few days in hospital and he'll bounce back as strong as ever."

"You look tired."

He massaged his hand across the back of his neck. "A little."

"I've made you sandwiches, and there's some scrumptious strawberry tarts Berta baked."

"That's very thoughtful."

She made a move toward the door. "I'll switch on the coffee."

"Don't worry about coffee."

She gestured toward the bar. "Can I get you a drink?"

"A cold beer would go down well."

She moved to the bar, and came up with a stubby of beer. She opened the bottle, grabbed a glass and brought it to him. He took the stubby from her proffered hand. "I'll just drink it straight from the bottle," he said and she placed the glass back on the bar.

He crossed to the table, sat down, and took a long and satisfying swig of the beer. Placing the bottle on the table, he wiped his mouth with the back of his hand.

She approached the table, and removing the protecting tablecloth and film wrap, moved the plate of sandwiches within his easy reach.

"Thanks," he said.

He ate in silence. Finally, he sat back, satisfied, smiling at her. "That hit the right spot." He tossed his napkin onto the table. "It's nice that you did this for me. Great that you stayed up and waited for me."

"My pleasure. Do you want anything else? Some fruit, perhaps, or some cheese and crackers?"

He patted his stomach lightly with one hand. "More than satisfied." He stood. "Will you wait here while I go up and see Sam?"

"I'll clear the table. Keep me busy."

"Won't be long," he said, and left the room.

• • •

As Joel climbed the stairs his mind filled suddenly and unexpectedly with thoughts of another woman—Madeleine, his wife, with her dark brown hair and soft hazel eyes.

Joel stood outside Sam's bedroom. Funny, but when he'd remembered Madeleine it hadn't been accompanied by the usual soul-tearing pain; maybe now he could talk openly about her and Gabriel for the first time since it happened.

He remembered Madeleine now with a tender feeling of love long tempered.

Maybe it had something to do with his desire for Cassie? He hadn't wanted a woman so much for as long as he could remember. Sex had always come easy to him; a trip into town, a drink or two with one of the local girls, a room at the pub and no promises. They understood his needs and their own. Could it be the same way with Cassie?

He hadn't changed his mind; he intended to keep Sam on Oriole because station life was best for the boy. It'd be preferable for Sam to grow up on the station, learn about station life until it became as natural to him as breathing. What could he learn in the city?

Cassie was warming to the idea of being on Oriole, and maybe he could convince her to allow Sam to stay because, like him, she wanted the best for her nephew.

He entered Sam's bedroom and, walking over to the sleeping child, stared down. No matter how many times he was with Sam, the boy astounded him. The upward curve of his mouth, the proud jut of his small chin, the way his black lashes swept over the top of his cheek.

Sam had entered his life and turned it upside-down. Joel was in awe of him. How could a little boy have such a profound effect on him?

Bending down, he kissed a flushed cheek. "Sleep well, Sam," he whispered. "Tomorrow and all your other tomorrows, I promise will hold adventures for you." He brushed a curl away from Sam's forehead. "I love you, Sam. Thanks for coming to me."

Fierce love for this tiny boy entered Joel's heart. He wanted to safeguard him from any mischief that dared come his way.

Tucking the sheet securely around the boy's shoulders, Joel quietly left the room, went downstairs and returned to Sam's aunt.

She was reading a *Time* magazine as he entered the room. Throwing down the magazine, she looked up at him. "Everything okay?"

"Yeah, he's sleeping like a kid."

"He is a kid." She laughed and, standing, walked toward the CD cabinet. Whilst tugging down a disc, a coin dropped and tinkled on to the polished floor. She reached down and retrieved it. "What's this?"

He stood beside her. "Well, well, where'd that come from? I haven't seen it in years." He took the coin from her. "It's an American dime from their Civil War period." He rubbed his finger over the coin. "They're extremely rare. My father brought it back from America for my mother, but we thought it'd got lost."

"Why would he bring her back a dime?"

"Dimes were used as love tokens. Their high silver content made them easy to engrave with lovers' initials or to pierce with small holes so that they might be added to jewelry or wrist chains. It was his way of telling her how much he loved her. That she was the only woman for him now and forever."

"That's so wonderful. Your father must have loved your mother very much."

His eyes misted over. What was he thinking about? Madeleine?

"Yeah, they had that special something."

She turned and replayed the CD. He took her into his arms, and slow danced with her. The music filled her mind.

"This music is made to order," he said.

Her body curved to his. Her softness melded against his hardness.

He buried his face into her hair, and whispered her name.

She nuzzled her lips behind his ear.

He tightened his grip. He was so strong—so utterly male—so real to her. She wanted the heat of love, the beat of love…no, no, no, sex. Sex was all she wanted from Joel.

"I want to talk about Sam." The dreamy bubble burst.

He took her hand and led her to the sofa where they sat. "What about Sam?"

"You see how he's settled in here. You must realize that this is the best place for him, a place where he'll grow up strong and protected."

His words were direct and she hated what he was saying to her because she knew he was right. Oriole offered Sam the best of lives. To take him back to Melbourne meant a crowded apartment, restricted to playing in parks, crèche when she was on an assignment. Joel offered a wonderful, clean life for a young child. She acknowledged this, yet how could she leave him? She wasn't strong enough to do such a thing. If only she were. If only she could say to Joel, yes, keep him here and protect him. Tears burned. "Are you going to take him from me?"

The tension between them increased with frightening intensity. "I want you to think about what's best for him."

"Being with me. That's what's best for him."

His curt voice lashed at her. "Best for him or for you!"

Cassie flinched. "I told you from the beginning that Sam stays with me. I'll never change my mind. Nothing you can do or say will make me give him up." She stood and looked down on him. "Don't get your hopes up, Joel. I won't let him stay here with you. When I leave, he's coming with me. You should be happy that I'll let him come for visits."

His lips puckered. "And if I'm not happy with that?"

She clenched her fists. "We've been here for over two weeks now, and I think maybe it would be in all our interests if we left for home tomorrow."

Standing, he towered over her. "What?"

She swallowed hard, lifted her chin, and boldly met his gaze. "I'm going back to Melbourne as soon as I can."

An unreadable expression on his face. It scared her. "That would be too hurtful for Queenie…" he hesitated, "and for me."

"I'm sure you can explain to your mother. You have such a way with words."

He touched her hand. She drew back. "Don't go. Not yet."
She hesitated. Unsure what to do. Her instincts told her to take
Sam and race back to Melbourne, her emotions told her to stay for
Queenie's sake and Sam's. He wouldn't understand them leaving
Oriole so quickly. He'd be so upset and God only knew what it
would do to Queenie's health to lose Sam before she'd got the chance
to know him. "You scare me, Joel, with your talk of keeping Sam."

Earnest eyes. Lying eyes. "Hey, I was just spouting off."

"Yet you admit you want Sam permanently on Oriole."

"Only if you agreed; I'll be content with visits."

She didn't believe him, yet she allowed her emotions to have
their way. "Okay."

Relief shone in his eyes. "Then you'll stay?"

"For a little while longer." What was going on in that devious
mind of his? Did he have a digit in the dial phoning his lawyer?
How could she fight him in court? He had the money, the power.
She had to be as devious as him.

"Great."

"But if you make one reference, make one move toward keeping
Sam, I'll be off this station so fast you'll feel my draught."

"I accede. He stays with you."

Cassie relaxed slightly. "We can work out suitable visits, Joel.
This can suit us all."

"Whatever."

"Why, when he leaves school he might want to come here
permanently," she conceded.

"Stranger things have happened."

Every player in this non-cooperative game had a set of possible
strategies on the table. Missiles launched. Summit over. For the moment.

"Good night, Cassie. Don't let the bed bugs bite." She watched
him walk out of the room and away from her.

"I can't let Sam go," she whispered to an empty room, and,
without warning, burst into tears.

CHAPTER THIRTEEN

A few days later, after a light lunch, Cassie and Sam found Queenie in the lounge. It was the first time Queenie had left her bedroom since they had arrived at Oriole. Pure pleasure washed through Cassie that Queenie's health had improved.

"Queenie." Cassie walked over to her and kissed her cheek. "How wonderful to see you up."

The older woman smiled. "Sam has been begging me to come downstairs. So here I am." Sam moved to cuddle close to her. "I promised that we'll read some stories in the garden and maybe plant some flowers, and then Sam wants to show me the horses."

"Please don't let him wear you out." Cassie knew too well how difficult it was to keep up with a boisterous four-year-old. "It would be unwise for you to do too much on your first day up and about."

They all turned as Berta made an appearance. "Joel said he's got something to show us."

To their utter surprise, Joel came into the room wearing a black cape and top hat. "Ah ha. Allow me to introduce myself." He gave a sweeping bow. "Bobo the Magician, and in honor of Sam's nana making her first public appearance downstairs in such a long time, I've come to do my special magic act."

Everyone clapped and cheered.

He winked at Cassie and turned to his captive audience. "Now for my Out to Lunch magic trick, taught to me by the Wizard of Fairy-tree Hill." Joel held up small sheets of paper. "I have here four pieces of paper and if you call out four names of fruit, I'll write them onto the paper."

"Apple," called Cassie.

"Pear," said Queenie.

"Banana," cried Sam.

"Grapes," came from Berta.

Joel filled a jar with the four pieces of paper. He approached Sam. "What's your name, little boy?"

Giggling, Sam got into the act. "Sam."

"Well, Sam, you are now going to tell us which piece of fruit is in the paper bag over there."

Sam pointed to his chest. "Me?"

Joel nodded. "You are now the magician's assistant. All you have to do is to pick a slip of paper and see what's drawn there. But first you must say the magic words: magic is great."

"Magic is great," Sam repeated solemnly, and, digging his hand deep inside the jar, he chose a piece of paper and cried out, "Apple."

Joel held up a paper bag. "Now, Sam, please remove the piece of fruit."

Sam removed the fruit from the paper bag, and proudly held up a rosy apple to the gasps of all. Everyone clapped loudly.

Joel took a bow with a flourish of one arm. "Now, ladies and gentleman, for my most remarkable trick of all." Sam selected a card from a deck of cards, which Joel showed his audience. He tore the card into pieces and placed it in a small metal bowl, the bowl was covered and when the cover was removed, Joel withdrew a string of silk scarves with the restored card on it. He placed the silk scarves back into the bowl. Raising his wand, he called, "abracadabra," whisked off the cover and the bowl was full of artificial flowers. Everyone roared their delight.

"That was great, Uncle Joel," Sam enthused. "Wasn't that good, Nana?"

"Hmm, I knew your Uncle Joel had many talents, but that wonderful act took me by surprise. Well done, Joel."

"Hey, Sam," Berta called, "Want to lick the bowl? I've made lamingtons and there's chocolate icing and coconut."

"Yippee," he cried, leaving his grandmother's side and hastening to take Berta's hand. He turned back. "Do you want me to bring you some chocolate icing, Nana?"

"No, dear, you eat it all, and when you're finished come back and tell me how great it was."

"Do you want a lamington, then?"

"That sounds delicious."

He gave a wave, and skipped out of the room with Berta. Queenie laughed.

Joel had moved to the other side of the room placing all his magic equipment into a cupboard. He turned pulling off his top hat as Cassie approached him. The blond curls tumbled down across his forehead. She reached over and brushed the curls back. "I can't believe this. You never told me you were a magician."

"What! And ruin my macho image."

"I want to know how you did the Out to Lunch trick."

He drew back, a horrified expression on his face. "Hey, no way. It's sacrilege for a magician to reveal his secrets. I took the Houdini oath."

"The Houdini oath?"

"Yeah, if I tell the secret of the Out to Lunch trick, I'll be kicked out of the magician club."

"Please tell me," she wheedled. "Just this one inconsequential trick."

He pursed his lips. "You're not an easy woman to say no to. Okay, but first you have to take the Houdini oath. Place your hand over your heart and swear, 'I'll never reveal the Out to Lunch trick for fear of never going out to lunch again.'"

Laughing, she did as he directed. "Satisfied?"

"Hmm. Can't be too careful with this lunch trick secret. Okay. The apple is in the bag from the start as I'm sure you realized. When you were all calling out the different fruit, I simply drew an apple on each piece of paper. Sam's prediction was a walk in the park from the inception."

Joel wanted nothing else but to make a little boy and a very sick lady smile.

"There's no end to my talents. See you both later," he said and left.

Laughing, Cassie approached Queenie. "I can't believe that Joel did such a wonderful thing. Your son is amazing."

"I'm forced to agree. Joel's giving Sam a horse. It will be good for him. Something of his own to care for, and also to teach him how to respect and care for animals."

Cassie sank back on to the armchair beside Queenie's chair. "He can't have a dog or cat in Melbourne, as we only have a tiny back garden and our apartment is quite small."

"I look at Sam and I feel such wonder that he has come into our lives. Such a little boy, and yet he's turned Oriole upside-down, and we wouldn't want it any other way." Queenie raised her hand to her chest. "Sam has stolen everyone's heart and especially mine."

Cassie understood exactly what she meant. "He has a way of doing that."

Both women stopped talking as Sam returned carefully balancing a plate holding the cake. His tongue popped out at the side of his mouth as he concentrated on carrying the plate to his grandmother. "Here's your lamington, Nana."

She took the plate, placing it on the small table at the side of her chair. She held out her arms, and Sam scrambled onto her lap. Queenie kissed his cheek. "Oh, Sam, I'm so much better since you've come to be with me. I hope you're going to stay here for a long, long time."

"I'm going to stay here for this much," he declared stretching out his arms. He glanced at Cassie. "Aren't we, Aunty C? We're going to stay forever and ever."

"I don't know about forever." At the deep frown on his face, she added, "But we'll stay for a while yet. Okay, Sam?"

Sam's welfare and happiness was the major priority in Cassie's life. When they returned to Melbourne, until school began at least, he could spend more time on Oriole. She knew how lonely she would become the times Sam left her, and even now, before the separation began, a stab of pain pricked at her heart.

Joel had to understand and accept that this was how it would be. There would be no debate. It would be better when she left Oriole; she'd most probably never see Joel again. Oh, there'd be telephone calls to discuss Sam's future and a general inquiry about her health but that would be the extent of her relationship with Joel.

Why did that make her feel so forlorn? As if she was losing her best friend? How deep were her feelings for Joel? Wasn't it all about sex and sex alone?

The walls were closing in on her. She had to get out of this house.

CHAPTER FOURTEEN

Cassie moved under the archway into the stable yards, glancing around as she did so. Everything as far as she could see was in tight order. The boxes were polished, the grass had been raked, and there was a silence around the place that seemed to glow with an atmosphere of tranquility.

A man in his late forties approached her. "Can I help you, miss?"

After she had explained to him what it was she wanted, he led a pure white mare from the stalls and saddled the horse.

Cassie ran an affectionate hand down the mare's neck, and breathed close to the horse's snout so it could familiarize itself with her. "She's beautiful. What's her name?"

"Moonlight. She's not as young as she used to be, but a smart lady and gentle as a lamb. She'll give you no trouble."

"Hi, Moonlight."

"I can come with you, if you want. Point out some of our highlights."

"Thanks, but no."

His face took on a concerned look. "The boss'll do me like a roast dinner if I let you go off ridin' on your own. He's given strict orders to keep an eye on you."

"I promise I won't go far. And I'll be back before Joel knows I'm gone." She raised three fingers of her right-hand. "Girl Scout's honor."

She edged the mare toward the fence boundaries, turning Moonlight on to the track that led away from the homestead.

The wind was hot and bit into her face like a blast from an open furnace.

Reaching the more open terrain, Cassie dug her heels into the horse's flanks gently urging her on, and finally they left the smoother area and entered rougher ground.

She was always a good rider but never a particularly daring one. This was her first time riding on uncultivated ground, but the mare was sure-footed. Cassie felt vitally alive and free.

She rode for about an hour, and then, almost exhausted, she dismounted and led the mare to a small creek. The horse lowered her massive head and drank the cool water. Rubbing her hand down the mare's flank, Cassie murmured, "Take it easy, girl. We'll rest for awhile."

She flung off her hat and knelt by the creek, splashing her burning face with water. She dipped her handkerchief into the creek, wrung it out, and tied it, bandanna-style, around her neck. The coolness of the cloth was soothing.

She sat beneath a tree. The next thing she knew, she awoke to the darkening sky. She must have slept for hours. Agitated, she sprang to her feet and raced to the mare. Alighting into the saddle, she patted the mare's neck. "Time to go back, Moonlight." She turned the horse in a half circle. In a gentle canter they headed back the way they had come.

It didn't take more than fifteen minutes for Cassie to realize she was hopelessly and completely lost. "I don't know where we are," she whispered and at the gentle whinny of the horse, said, "Don't worry, girl. I know you'll get us home."

She glanced around her at the ever-darkening bush. She shivered. "Somehow."

Cassie searched for anything that was familiar. The trees swayed as if in some macabre dance. The wind whistled a mournful tune through the branches and leaves.

It would only be a matter of time before she was found.

The horse stumbled. Cassie lurched precariously in the saddle. With one hand, she tightly gripped the saddle pommel, her heart thumping wildly in her breast.

She had no water. In the morrow's heat, she wouldn't last more than a day. She should have stayed by the creek.

The rush of terror almost overcame her. No matter how hard she tried, she couldn't hold back her labored breathing.

"Okay, I have a right to be frightened, because this is scary."

She drew the mare to a halt, searching the darkness for a cave, some place of shelter.

A sudden flash of lightning illuminated a horse and rider on the crest of a hill ahead of her. Cassie choked back a gasp of relief, too afraid to allow herself to hope they were real.

The horse reared its front legs high into the air at his rider's command to halt.

A black silhouette of man and beast set against a background of silver lightning.

Apart from the wind tossing the stallion's mane and lifting the tail of his mountain man's coat, man and beast could have been carved from the very earth upon which they stood.

And they were as real as she. She gave a harsh sob as she allowed an overpowering sense of relief to flood her. She edged the mare forward, halting a few feet away from him.

Joel, astride a black stallion, with his Akubra tugged low over his eyes, looked magnificent. She likened him to a vindicating archangel who had been sent to earth to proclaim it his. She whispered his name and it flew like an eagle with the wind into the endless night.

"Thank God, I've found you," he yelled above the roar of thunder. He edged his stallion until their horses' flanks touched. "I was out of my mind with worry."

"Oh, Joel, I'm so sorry. I didn't mean to cause such concern. I didn't think about getting lost. I thought I knew exactly how to get back."

He scooped his arm around her waist and dragged her against him. He kissed her as if it were their first kiss, as if it were their last. She parted her lips for him, sliding forward in her saddle. The rain beating upon her face tasted as sweet as his mouth.

He whipped a coat from his saddlebag and tossed it over her shoulders. "Here, put this on before you catch your death."

She struggled into the coat. "I thought you'd never find me. I was so scared."

He leaned forward in his saddle. "The main thing is that you're safe. Don't go against me again, Cassie. I warned you not to go alone in the bush. My God, even experienced men become disorientated and lost before they know it."

"It won't happen again."

"Too damn right it won't happen again. I'll make sure of that. I specifically warned you about the dangers of the outback, and bloody hell, you went straight ahead and disobeyed me."

"I'm sorry, Joel. Truly, I am."

He seemed a little appeased. "You didn't give a thought about Sam or Queenie or…or any of us."

He took the lead, and, like a lamb to slaughter, Cassie followed meekly behind.

•••

Through the mud and slime being kicked into the air by the horse's hooves, Cassie could see the homestead. Joel halted and swung from the saddle. He lifted Cassie down but instead of placing her on her feet swung her over one shoulder like a sack of potatoes. One big hand slipped under her coat, he clutched her backside and carried her through the relentless rain toward the house.

A stockman approached him. "Everything okay, boss?"

"Fine, Bert. Look after the horses, will you?"

Joel kicked open the front door with his boot, then proceeded up the stairs and into his bedroom. He sat her on the edge of the bed and removed her raincoat.

"I want to see Sam."

"Later."

"No, now, Joel. I want to see him and your mother. They must be worried about me."

He gave a grim laugh. "You could say that." He went to the chest of drawers and rummaging through came out with an oversized sweater. "Hold up your arms." She obeyed without question, relishing the warmth of the wool as it slid over her shivering shoulders. "Thanks."

"Make it quick. Your lips are blue and your hair's sticking out in frozen clumps."

"Gee thanks, I was feeling okay until you put me right."

She left him and went into Sam's room. He was tucked into his bed, his pajamas clean and crisp. He was looked after here at Oriole as well as she could have.

Sam tugged her sleeve. "Hi," she said.

"You got lost in the rain," he declared. His bottom lip pouted. "And I wanted you home here with me, but you didn't come."

"I know. I'm such a silly billy. I just couldn't find my way back."

"Uncle Joel found you, didn't he, Aunty C?"

"He did." She touched her lips to her nephew's cheek.

Sam's eyes brightened with mischief. "He came on his big black horse and he said, 'I've found you, Aunty C.'"

"And I said, 'Oh, Uncle Joel, I've been so scared until you came for me.'"

"And he said, 'Well, I've found you now and I love you too much to leave you in the rain by yourself.'"

"Yes, he did."

"What did you say to him?"

"I said 'Thanks, Uncle Joel.'"

He shook his head impatiently. "No, you said, and I love you too, Uncle Joel."

Her throat closed over and she wondered why. "Oh, yes, that's right. I did say that."

"Nana cried and so did Uncle Joel, but I didn't. I knew you'd come home soon."

Had he? Had Joel cried when she was lost and alone in the bush? Or was it just a young child's ramblings? She kissed Sam's rosy cheek again. "Do you know how much I love you?"

"Yep," he murmured and outstretched his tiny arms. "This much."

Rising from the bed, she leaned over and ran a finger down the lush warmth of his satin smooth skin. His Buzz Lightyear cuddled beside him, one tiny arm thrown protectively over the doll. She leaned down and placed a gentle kiss on the side of his mouth. "Sleep tight, sweetheart," she whispered.

She made a brief visit to Queenie who, so glad to see Cassie, hugged her tight. Once assured that Cassie was alive and kicking, Queenie allowed her to leave.

Back in his bedroom, Joel was playing an instrument similar to a xylophone. Their gaze met and he smiled. "Hi. I'm keeping in practice."

"Practice? It sounds awful."

He showed her the instrument. "It's a Marimba, a primitive African xylophone. In fact the modern orchestral instrument evolved from this." His laugh was low, throaty. "Another piece of useless information for you."

"I'll write it up in my useless information book."

Placing the instrument carefully on the floor, he approached her. "You look beat."

"I feel as though I've mustered an entire herd."

"Hold up your arms," he ordered gently. Tired, and desperately needing to sleep for hours, she obeyed. With one deft movement, he removed the sweater along with her T-shirt.

"Lean forward."

Her nose buried into his chest, the warmth of him tingled her skin. His musky odor overwhelmed her senses. She loved his smell. She loved the power of him and knew that as long as she was with him no harm could ever come to her.

His hands fumbled with the hooks of her bra. The bra joined her shirt on the floor. He knelt in front of her and removed her shoes, vigorously rubbing her feet until her tingling toes changed from blue to bright red. Standing, he said, "Stand up."

He tugged the elastic of her shorts. She placed her hand over his. "Don't, I can do it."

"Leave off," he said and tugged harder.

She clung on tighter. The elastic pinged. "I'll do it. You turn around."

"What don't you want me to see?"

"My Bridget Jones panties. They're comfortable for riding."

"So what?"

"I look so great in my black bikini."

"I don't doubt it."

"I don't want you disappointed."

"Give off, Cassie." And with one hefty tug he jerked down her shorts and panties. She stepped out of them. Naked. Nipples peaked. Goosebumps paraded across her skin like Braille. Bugger, this wasn't what she had in mind—she'd wanted slinky, seductive, him panting at the bit, that sort of thing.

He looked down. She'd shaped her pubes into a strip. He grinned. "Landing strip?"

She grinned. "Need ground control?"

"I've never needed directions."

She trembled as his fingers traced the curve of her spine, his other hand resting lightly on one hip. "You're freezing." He wrenched a cotton blanket from the bed and wrapped it around her. "Wait here."

Taking deep breaths, Cassie endeavored to gain control of her emotions and her chattering teeth. She heard the sound of running water. He returned to her. "I'll look after you."

Her body jerked when his hand brushed against her thigh. "What?" she mumbled. "What did you say?"

"I'll massage your neck and shoulders. It'll get your blood circulating. You'll be warm in no time."

He sat on the bed slightly behind her. His hands strong but gentle as they pressed into the sore muscles of her shoulders.

Her head fell forward as his fingers threaded through her hair. Rubbing. Stroking. Grazing. *Please God, don't let me drool.*

The feel of his skin beneath her fingers made heat explode deep in Cassie's belly and desire, as old as time, captured her.

He shifted until he faced her. She brushed her mouth across the soft curve of his cheek. She sucked in the lush fullness of his bottom lip. Electric sensations flowed in the most necessary places at the luminous glow of his eyes.

He brushed the tip of his tongue across an eyelid. He tightened his arms around her, pulling her down on top of him. The blanket fell away. His arms entwined around her waist; she wrapped her arms around his neck and kissed him all over his face, neck, and chest, sucking his nipple.

He needed no further invitation. His hand explored the lines of her back, her waist, and her hips, while she caressed the length of his back.

His passionate kiss…Demanding. Total. It filled her with an amazing sense of completeness.

He spun her beneath him. Their lips joined in a kiss of such unutterable sweetness, a wave of tenderness, and another deeper sensation, one she couldn't fathom, a strange sweet feeling that swept over her like the gentle hush of a mountain breeze.

His hand slid down to grasp hers.

The sounds of the night echoed. The wind swaying through the trees. A soft hoot of a barn owl. Out in the hall, the tick of the tall grandfather clock. Yet she knew nothing except him.

"I think the bath's full. I'd better go and turn off the taps or we'll be swimming."

As he left the room, she called, "I like it hot."

"Yes, ma'am."

"And plenty of bubbles."

"Yes, ma'am."

He returned and scooped her into his arms, and carrying her into the bathroom, he lowered her into a steaming bath smelling of lavender. Such caveman antics left her breathless.

She'd always taken control. If she'd fancied a guy, she'd ask him out. If she wanted him in her bed, she'd take the initiative. But here now with Joel, she didn't know, she just didn't know. Her barriers, her defenses she'd built up over the years were shattering and she didn't know what to do about it.

He knelt and, lifting a sponge, bathed her with gentle strokes of his hand. Cassie's head dropped back on to the rim of the bath, her eyes closed.

"Lean forward." He ran the water through her hair. Adding shampoo, he massaged her scalp with strong strokes. Erotic. Pleasurable. A sensation beyond sensation. He rinsed her hair clean and pushed her back against the tub.

She offered him no resistance. Wanting him to take control.

He lifted her from the water, towel dried her, wrapped her in a huge terrycloth robe and, carrying her to the bed, lowered her on it.

He leaned down and kissed her mouth. Warm, so totally warm. Her body snuggled into the deepness of the mattress. She was sinking lower and lower.

His hands were everywhere now. Wonderful. Exciting and so warm. "Oh, yes," she muttered. "Yes. Ye-s. Yess-sss—z-z-zzzzzzzzzzz."

•••

Cassie bolted upright. "What!" She glanced at the luminous clock. Six. Her hand spread over the other side of the bed. Where was Joel? What had happened? Had they made love? She hit her forehead with the heel of her hand. "I fell asleep. While the man was making love to me I snored off."

Humiliation upon humiliation. How could she have fallen asleep? Why did he not wake her?

"Bugger."

Showered and dressed, Cassie moved downstairs. Joel was in the kitchen drinking coffee. He smiled when he saw her; she cringed inside.

"Are you somewhat restored after your ordeal?"

"Greatly."

"Nasty experience being lost in the bush. One I'm thankful to say I haven't experienced."

"And not one I care to repeat."

"Don't go out riding on your own again. Okay?" He cocked his head to one side. "I don't want anything to happen to you."

"Don't you?"

"No. I want you safe and sound and with me."

"That sounds nice."

"So you'll do as you're told?"

She saluted. "Sir. Yes, sir," she promised as she sat in a chair next to him.

"With everything that's happened to you since you arrived here, you'll be glad to leave Oriole."

"Oh, I don't know. I'm getting used to all the excitement."

He grinned. "I would have argued that the outback was safer than the city."

"None of it was your fault."

"I want to protect you—and Sam."

"I can't tell you how happy Sam is here at Oriole. It's as if he's lived here all his life."

"This is his home."

She wanted to question this statement and say that this wasn't his home. His home was with her in Melbourne. She dismissed the idea. Now was not the time. "You're his hero."

"I rather like that role. I hope I never do anything to change his mind about me."

"I doubt that you ever could."

"Thanks for saying that." He turned back to the stove. "Bacon and eggs coming up." He turned his head slightly. "We'll leave for our camping trip in the morning."

"It's a wonder you still want me to go."

He chuckled, his back now to her. "Aw, I don't know, seems to me you make things um, well, interesting."

Should she bring up last night? Apologize? God, no, he must think she played for laughs now without adding fuel to fire.

Let them act like nothing untoward had happened between them. All politeness and light. And that's the way she intended to keep it.

CHAPTER FIFTEEN

Cassie stretched her legs down the bed. She had been surprised and pleased when Joel had talked about their camping trip. She wasn't sure why, but she'd imagined, after her little girl lost routine, he would change his mind and not want her to go with them. Yet he'd told her that he was making plans for them to leave early today, before the heat of the day made travelling far too unbearable.

She woke before dawn with a feeling of intense excitement. Like when she was a kid and the day had held some special treat in store for her—a birthday or Christmas.

Could this feeling of excitement come from the fact that she would be alone with Joel and things between them may progress beyond a kiss? Bloody hell, was she a masochist? Hadn't she made a vow of chastity where Joel was concerned? And here she was planning her next jump-his-bones.

She turned on to her back and stared up at the grey shadows streaking across the white ceiling of her room.

Swinging back the sheet, she padded to the shower. By seven, she had packed their gear. Lugging their overnight bags, she trailed Sam downstairs. She left their bags near the front door. Taking Sam by the hand they went into the kitchen. Berta was moving about the room preparing breakfast, and it flashed through Cassie's mind that no matter how early she rose, Berta was always up before her.

Cassie lifted Sam on a bar stool as Berta placed a bowl of cornflakes, milk, and chopped banana in front of him. "Eggs and bacon, Cassie?" she inquired.

Cassie shook her head. "Thanks, but no thanks. Toast and coffee will be fine."

"We're going camping, Berta," Sam said, swallowing a mouthful of cereal.

"Heard that, Sam," Berta answered, placing a mug of steaming coffee in front of Cassie.

He pushed out a foot. "I've got on my new boots that my Uncle Joel bought me and they came on the plane with Bluey."

Berta smiled and studied the proffered foot. "Hmm, wish I had me a pair of those boots, then I don't reckon my feet would ache as much."

"Aunty C can get you some, can't you, Aunty C? You can have the same color as me, can't she, Aunty C?"

Cassie laughed. "If Berta wants. Be quiet now, Sam, and finish your breakfast."

The door of the kitchen flew open and Joel stood there surveying the scene in front of him.

The sunlight, pouring through an open window, danced on the lushness of his hair. Her gaze fixed to his and her heart locked in her chest.

"Want another cup of coffee, Cassie?"

"What?"

"Coffee. You know the stuff you drink." She gave a deep chuckle. "Or have you forgotten the ordinary things of life?"

She flashed Berta an annoyed look. She didn't need her wicked humor so early in the morning, but her heart sank a little in her chest that maybe Berta was seeing right through her, knew what she was thinking.

"Don't know what you're talking about, Berta. And no coffee, thanks."

"Ready?" Joel asked.

She nodded, slid off the stool. "I left our luggage near the—"

"In the back of the car already." He looked at Sam. "Ready?" he asked. Sam's whoop of delight was deflated by Cassie telling him to clean his teeth.

A few minutes later they left the house and made their way to Joel's Toyota Camry parked in the driveway.

He opened the front passenger side door for Cassie, secured Sam in his booster chair in the back and slid behind the steering wheel. "Okay, we're on our way for the adventure of a lifetime." He looked over at Cassie, "Navigator ready?"

Cassie gave a quick salute. "Ready and able, sir."

Joel glanced back at Sam. "Animal and bird spotter, ready?"

Sam gave a stiff salute. "Ready and able, sir."

The car roared into life. "Then let's go bush."

They travelled along the Great Northern Highway until they reached Fitzroy Crossing, then another twenty kilometers northeast to Geikie Gorge, formed by centuries of water eroding through an ancient limestone reef.

"It's a good source of fresh water and there are all sorts of fish, birds, and other animals," Joel told them as they drove deep into the magnificent gorge.

She drew in her breath at the multi-colored cliffs reflected in the placid waters of the Fitzroy River, which flowed through the gorge.

Joel pulled up at the side of the road. They left the car and lifting Sam high upon his shoulders, Joel insisted they climb to the top of a massive hill. He waved his hand across the space between them. "Welcome to my Shangri-La," he expounded.

Camera slung around her neck, Cassie held up her hand for him to stay where he was. She took several shots until he said enough.

Cassie drank in the breathtaking view of the surrounding spectacular limestone cliffs. "Joel, oh it's truly beautiful."

Joel gently tugged one of Sam's legs. "What do you think, Tiger? Bit of all right?"

The boy untangled the fingers that were gripping Joel's hair and clapped his tiny hands. "It's real beaut, Uncle."

"I didn't realize Australia was so beautiful," Cassie whispered linking her gaze with his.

"There's much more to come," he promised.

• • •

It was late afternoon when they arrived at a mangrove-fringed estuary where he decided they would set up camp. A flock of pink and white galahs greeted them wildly on their arrival. The immediate area was filled with wild flowers—red and green kangaroo paw, vivid blue leschenaultias, and dryandras with their large, spiky flowers.

Joel unpacked their gear and set up camp, throwing orders in her direction every few minutes. She was pleased to help. He laughed when Sam got into the act and carried the smaller things, such as the tin billy for making tea, their backless wooden and cloth-seated camp chairs, and the first-aid kit.

I'll make us something to eat," Joel suggested and moved with Sam to the back of the car.

Cassie wandered around, taking in her surroundings but not allowing Sam to be out of her sight. It certainly was a pleasant place to camp.

"Uncle Joel has made us some sandwiches," Sam called to her.

She joined them, and sat on a campstool next to Sam.

Joel spoke to Cassie. "Hungry?"

"Starving." She placed her hat on top of a large boulder and eagerly accepted the sandwich Joel was offering her. It was large enough to feed an army. "It's huge."

Joel's eyes crinkled at the corners. "A Murrumbidgee sandwich."

She made sure her eyes grew wide and round. "And what's a Murrumbidgee sandwich when it's at home?"

The crinkles deepened. "According to the locals, it's a wild pig between two bags of flour."

They laughed.

"Want some good, old-fashioned billy tea?" he asked.

She shook her head slightly. "Is there anything cool to drink?"

"Water."

"Water will be fine."

Finally, when they'd finished their meal, Joel suggested a game of makeshift cricket using a plastic ball and small wooden bat.

Cassie moved away from the game area and proceeded to sit on a rather large boulder.

"Come and play, Aunty C," Sam called.

Joel looked across at her. How handsome he looked against the harshness of the wild bush background. Even from this distance, she could see the dark blue of his eyes, the cool, rugged beauty of his face with its touch of sadness.

A feeling washed through her. A wonderfully nice feeling. Oh, my God, was she falling in love with him? How easy it would be to love him. Forget there was a barrier between them and allow love to have its way.

"Come on, Aunty C. You can be the fielder," Joel added with a grin, as she obliged them. They played for an hour.

It was becoming hotter by the second. She needed a bath or a swim or whatever one did to get clean and cool when completely isolated deep within the Australian bush.

The river looked cool and so inviting. She got her camera from the car. Good time to take some shots for Jane. She glanced around. There was a myriad of water birds—coots clambering through the river vegetation, bustards, and marsh crake. The river was interspersed with floating weeds and water lilies.

A wallaby poked his nose out of the bushes, sniffed the air, then hopped back to his habitat, and a feeling of serenity overcame her as the stillness of the outback engulfed her. It was like being transported into nature's fairyland, and suddenly she felt the same passion for the bush that Joel possessed. Through his eyes, she saw the magnificent colors, and the sheer wonderment of the Australian bush.

She spun around to tell him of the phenomenon she had experienced; her pulse beat in her throat. Joel had stripped down to his khaki shorts, his well-developed muscles rippling beneath his sun-bronzed skin at every movement he made. Threaded through the leather belt strapped around his waist was a mean-looking sheathed bowie knife. Her camera clicked and clicked.

She walked over to the fire. "You look like Tarzan."

His smile came from somewhere deep within him. She felt as light-hearted, and as young as her years.

"You sure you don't mean Cheetah?"

She laughed. "Cheetah was one very cute chimp."

His eyes slid down her body. "You can be my Jane any day."

She took a step closer to him, and his big hand reached out to her. "I don't have a sarong."

"You'd look good in anything. Or nothing."

"Uncle, Uncle Joel, lift me up." He lifted the boy into his arms. "Can I go for a swim, Uncle Joel?"

"Is it safe?" Cassie asked.

"Safe as houses," Joel assured her and lowered Sam to his feet.

She took Sam's hand. "Watch where you walk," she warned him. "There could be snakes."

"Don't make him afraid of nature, Cassie."

"He doesn't understand the nature of the bush yet," she insisted.

"That's the whole idea of this trip. To observe the bush and its inhabitants," Joel said.

"I'm keeping my eye on him all the time."

Joel grinned. "Yes, ma'am." He looked down at the boy. "Aunty's right, Sam. Watch where you walk, always be alert. and remember that this is their home not ours, so we must treat the bush with respect."

"And not kick them or anything," Sam said.

"Too right," Joel said.

"Perhaps you can help me get over my aversion to creepy crawlies along the way," Cassie said.

"I think you're a lost cause."

She lifted her shoulders. "I'll try to be braver."

"It'll come. Give yourself time."

She scrambled inside the car and dug deep inside her bag until she found her green-and-white striped one-piece bathing suit. Dragging the curtains across the windows of the car, she took off her clothes, struggled into her bathers, and, slipping her feet into her white canvas shoes, grabbed Sam's bathers and two towels and climbed from the car.

It was a wonderful, glorious day. Cassie delighted in the heat on her bare head. Galahs swept through the brilliant blue sky dipping their wings before soaring up into the high, protective branches of the eucalyptus gum.

She stripped Sam down and helped him into his bathers.

They walked to the river's edge. She knelt down and tested the water with her hand. "Perfect." She glanced down at her nephew and taking him by the hand, cried, "Ready, set, go." They fell laughing into the cool, invigorating water. For such a long while, they splashed about in happy contentment.

"It's getting late," Joel called. Reluctantly, they made their way out of the water. "Come on, Tiger, and I'll help you dress while Aunty C changes out of her wet bathers."

Later, worn-out but exhilarated, they sat on the camp chairs. Sam curled up on Joel's lap. He kissed the top of the boy's halo of sandy curls.

What a great day this had been.

Night came quickly, and Joel lit a fire and barbecued sausages, eggs, and tomatoes over the flames. Unable to resist the temptation to show off, he flipped the eggs high with a spatula, catching them on the downward turn.

"Hungry, Sam?"

"Yep," he answered, not stifling the yawn that stretched his tiny mouth.

"And tired, too, I think," said Cassie. "It's been a long day for him."

"I've made up his bed in the back of the car. Don't want him to wake up in the middle of the night and get scared," Joel said, flashing a grin. "Wouldn't want him growing up scared of anything that slivers."

"Thanks for sharing that with me, Doctor Spock."

It was the way he looked at her that gave Cassie the sensation of floating away into the atmosphere. The glorious day, the three of them together alone in the bush was magical. With all her strength she wished for this to be real and that they would become a real family. "Don't look at me like that."

His brows rose in innocent surprise. "Like what?"

"Like I was a strawberry sundae and you haven't tasted ice cream for a year."

"Okay."

"Okay what?"

"Okay, I'll hide my eyes, that way you won't know where I'm looking—or how." He lifted his mountain man's hat from the ground and, placing it on his head, pulled it down until the brim covered his eyes. "Better?"

Sam giggled. "Uncle Joel, you won't be able to see anything," he cried, tugging Joel's shirtsleeve.

"Aunty C doesn't like my eyes."

Sam scratched his head. "Why?"

"Because."

"'Cos why?" Sam demanded.

"'Cos of this," Joel cried whipping off his hat and pulling a weird face at Sam, who immediately fell into a fit of the giggles.

"Your Uncle Joel is wasting his talents, Sam," Cassie placed her hands on her hips. "He should be on the stage."

"The first one out of town," Joel said, and this time they all fell into peals of laughter.

Joel noticed Sam was toying with the remainder of his food. "Don't you want any more tucker, Sam?"

The child shook his head. "I'm full up to here," he said indicating the beginning of his neck.

He glanced over at Cassie. "How about I put him to bed while you finish your dinner?"

She nodded her thanks. She held out her arms and Sam raced into them. She enclosed him into her arms. "Do you know how much I love you?"

Pulling back from his Aunty C, he outstretched his arms. "This much."

She smothered his face with her kisses. "Good night sweetheart. Sleep tight."

"Night, Aunty C," he said, and a yawn stretched his mouth. "See you in the morning."

Joel lifted Sam into his arms. "Come on, Tiger, I'll help you get ready for bed." He hoisted the child high until he was standing on his shoulders. Joel secured his hands around the back of Sam's legs.

"Look, Aunty C," he cried, his voice filled with excitement, "I'm bigger than my uncle."

"Yes, you are, Sam." She made a great show of craning her neck to see his face.

Sam's chest swelled with pride. "When I grow up I'm going to be just like my uncle."

"What do you think about that, Aunty C?" Joel whispered.

I think that if he was only a little like you, he'd be one of the best men around. If she had to choose a role model, then Joel would be it. Oh, how much she wanted Sam to grow up with the same values, the solid strength, and integrity that his Uncle Joel displayed. "He could do worse."

"Come on, Tiger, time for bed."

He returned some minutes later sitting across from her on the other side of the fire. "Can you believe it? He was asleep before I took his shoes off!" He laughed. "He's amazing." He picked up a log of wood and tossed it on the fire. Sparks flew, dancing around the flames.

"He's had a lot of excitement." She glanced at him and turned her gaze to the flames. *The same as me, but my excitement comes from just being with Joel.* "He's enjoying this trip enormously."

He ran a hand through his hair, and that same ever-straying, solitary lock fell over his forehead. She resisted the near-uncontrollable urge to lean over and brush the lock back, and the truth descended on her, and she knew, beyond all doubt, that she was in love with Joel—loved him with every beat of her heart.

Oh this was so not what she wanted. Kissing, yes. Sex, too, bloody right. Love—oh, my God, no.

"And his aunt?"

"I'm loving it," she said.

"I fell in love with Oriole the first time I saw it." He stretched his long legs out in front of him. "I hadn't long been back from Africa and found the confines of Sydney too restrictive. I needed space. I went searching for a property and found Oriole."

"And you included your family in this venture?"

"My family is very important to me." He dug at the dirt with the heel of one boot. "My brother and his wife didn't take to station life. They lasted about a year and then high-tailed it back to Sydney. After their divorce, Luke moved to Melbourne when he was offered work there."

"And met Claudia."

He nodded. "Fate."

Needing to clear the air between them, she said, "Do you hate her? My sister—do you resent her for what she did to Luke?"

She waited for him to accuse her of not believing him at the beginning about Luke being the innocent in the affair. Of calling him a liar. Instead, he said, "No, I don't. I believe in fate." Leaning back, he hooked his thumbs inside the waistband of his jeans. "What must be will be, that sort of thing."

She needed now to tell him the truth about Claudia. "My sister was wild. An uncontrollable girl. My parents indulged her and when they died, I took up the reins and continued giving her everything she wanted." She leaned forward her elbows on her knees. "I truly don't think she meant to hurt anyone. It was a game to her. A game that went wrong when she discovered she was pregnant with Sam."

His smile was an intimate as a caress. "Then we can let that part of our lives die a natural death?"

"Yes, yes I guess we can." She didn't speak for a short time, and then said to him, "Your mother told me about Madeleine and your baby."

A raised eyebrow. "It was a long time ago."

"But still painful, I should imagine."

Hesitation. A long sigh. "Yes, it hurts a little when I think about them for too long. I suppose that will always be there. The regrets, the idea of the could-have-beens. The type of man my son would have grown into."

Almost too scared of his answer, she asked the question that had been preying on her mind. "You loved Madeleine very much, didn't you?"

His eyes reflected golden lights from the fire. A small wind blew up from nowhere and flirted around his hair, teasing it, bidding the blond curls to dance at its command. The radiance from the fire enhanced his eyes, making the bronze of his skin dazzle.

"We were both young and eager. It seems such a long time ago now. I thought I'd never get over losing her, but now—" He shrugged. "I don't know, it's like I can place them here," he tapped his heart, "where they're safe and get on with living."

"She would want that. She would want you to get on with your life."

He smiled at her and her heart skipped a beat. "Yeah, I know she would."

A comfortable silence. "I'm surprised it isn't colder," she said after a while.

"It'll get colder later," he told her.

His look, which came to her across the fire-lit space, bamboozled and spellbound her. It brought her to heights she had never before experienced. It crashed her down to earth in a confused heap. He was mystifying, unexplainable, and wonderfully male.

He hit a falling log with the heel of his boot and sparks shot up into the sky like an exploding firecracker. "After my wife and son died, I thought I'd never love again, never have a family. So that made me believe I was the last of the Caine family, and then I learned about Sam. It nearly blew my mind."

Even in the fast growing dusk, as he spoke, she could see his eyes become jewel-colored. Sam was the eternal link that would hold them together for all time. Bound together by a silken cord.

"I want everything good for him. I want to be good for him."

Through the stillness of the darkening bush, she said, "I couldn't imagine you to be anything else to him."

"This trip has been good for the three of us," he said. "I feel sort of…aw, closer to you somehow. We needed this time together."

"I guess we did, Joel."

His face was inscrutable, eerily lit by the dancing tips of fire. Alone with Joel in this magical night with so many stars, she wanted him to scoop her into his arms and sweep her into a sky opaque enough to dance across.

As if sensing her need, he left his post and took a position sitting beside her. Their gazes locked. She lowered hers first. Her head tilted forward as she reached over to pick up a piece of fallen branch.

She hadn't realized he had moved until he was kissing the soft skin of her neck. A desire that was all potent. all consuming filled her. Her limbs melted and her heart thumped wildly in her chest.

Her heart quickened at his touch, and she wanted his kisses with a raw emotion that sent her senses reeling.

He moved his mouth until it rested in the indentation of her chin and then to press lightly on top of hers. His tongue moved around the inside of her mouth. Warm, exciting.

He tasted like sweet, heady wine. His skin was smooth, his mouth hot.

He wrapped his arms around her, and desire flooded her. She was fast losing control.

She heard him whisper her name and she pulled back from him. He brought his hand to box the back of her head. His lips still pressed to hers, he murmured, "Want a cup of tea?"

She brushed her lips across his. "No."

"Want I should make you coffee?"

She giggled. "No coffee."

"Do you want to go dancing?"

Drawing back from his mouth, she laughed gleefully. "You idiot."

He cupped her chin and stroked her cheek with his thumb. "You must be tired and we've an early start in the morning."

He moved away from the firelight and walked toward the car. "Joel!"

"What?"

Apprehension slithered in her belly. "Where are you going?"

"Getting our swags."

"Hurry. It's getting so damn dark."

He returned and threw a log on to the fire. "In a few moments you won't be able to see your hand in front of you," he said.

The bush around her had darkened to the point that the trees stood out in black relief. Her earlier feeling of ease had vanished and in its place was an ever-growing dread.

Vulnerable, her mind conjured up witches' claws, wild animals that bit and scratched and stung their poison, and—she shuddered—slithering creatures that wound their way around your body and squeezed and squeezed until you didn't have a breath of air left inside your lungs.

Goosebumps rose on her arms. She brought a hand to her throat. Panic fluttered. *Gain control.* Nothing could harm her. Joel was here to look after her. But all the self-talk did nothing to alleviate her fears.

A rustle in the bush behind her caused her to spin around. She strained her ears to hear. Noises seemed to come from all directions. A wail from deep inside the bushes, a hoot over there behind a tree, and the slithering sound of a deadly brown snake rustling through the leaves and dirt. A snake that could kill you with one venomous bite.

She trembled, and her heart beat at such a furious rate. Was she having a minor heart attack?

Where in the hell was Joel?

Another sound invaded her mind—the sound of sanity and she realized Joel was speaking to her. "What?"

Except for the fire, it was now total black. She reached out and grabbed his jeans, clinging on for dear life.

"I said the first time in the bush is always the worst."

Now that Joel was with her, she was much calmer. Her heart fell into a soft thud and the buzz in her head dropped to an even drone.

She tightened her grip of his pants. "Let go of my jeans," he said.

"Why, where are you going?" she demanded.

He laughed. "Nowhere. I want to fix your sleeping bag."

Reluctantly, she released her hold, standing and moving in close to him. He nearly knocked her over as he spread out her sleeping bag.

Even though he said, "Move off. I can't concentrate," he curled his arm around her waist.

"Sorry," she murmured. "I'm just a yellow-bellied coward at heart."

As he kissed her mouth, she drew quickly away from him. Ignoring the throb of her heart, the craving to taste more of his mouth.

"Glad to play the hero."

"Do we have ground sheets?" Even to her own ears, her voice sounded tiny.

"Ground sheets?"

"Please."

"I'll get you one, okay?"

The chill of being alone cascaded her mind as if someone had thrown ice water over her head. She grabbed his arm. "On second thought, please don't bother." She glanced anxiously at the fire. "You'll keep the fire going all night?"

"What do you suggest? That we take two-hour shifts?"

Refusing to move as much as an inch away from him, she said, "Sarcasm is the lowest form of wit."

"Yeah, but the highest form of entertainment." He let out a heavy sigh. "The fire will die out eventually and there's nothing I can do about that."

"Are there snakes?"

"Yes."

A shiver. "Can they get into the sleeping bag with you?"

"Only if you're silly enough to leave it unzipped."

A frown. "You can be crass at times."

He was chuckling as he turned and disappeared. His outline shadowed on the other side of the fire.

She had no intention of taking off so much as a sock. Too vulnerable. Sliding into the sleeping bag, she zipped it up and cuddled down into its soft warmth. She would never sleep. Not here in the open with all those horrible creepy-crawlies out there.

She willed her eyes closed. *Okay, okay, relax. You're becoming neurotic. You're going to be fine. Everything's okay...*She heard a rustling sound in the bush behind her. Her body tensed. She strained her ears, spelling backwards at the speed of sound. She heard the trees whisper strange and exotic tales to each other, and her heart pounded loudly in her ears. There it was again, that rustling sound as if some slimy creature was slithering its way through the bush towards its target—her!

"Joe—lll," she shouted, sitting up as best she could with the restriction of the sleeping bag. He never answered her. She screamed his name. "Joel!"

"What?"

"Something's in the bush behind me." Was he deaf? Anyone with minimal hearing could hear it.

"No kidding."

"It could be a s-s-snake." She hated even uttering the word. It made it seem more likely and more real.

"Go to sleep."

"But...but—"

This time it was an order. "Go to sleep."

She screwed her eyes tight, wriggling her way down the bag as far as she could. If she were to be bitten to death by some ghastly adder then she would prefer not to see it happen.

Her heart thudded wildly in her chest; she was as taut as a violin string.

Everyone had his or her own special fears. Some people couldn't climb a ladder. And what about those who turned pale when they had to use an elevator? Or feared spiders or dogs—the list went on. Okay, so her aversion was to anything that had to slither on its stomach to be mobile.

Was that a sin? Did it make her the odd woman out? So she had a weakness. Well, with a little spunk and tenacity she could overcome this fear. Why, she could —

A heavy thud on her legs. She tried to sit up. The thing moved. It was a snake. She'd die a horrible death.

"Oh, hell…oh, hell…oh, oh, oh—"

The scream began at the base of her throat then ripped out with such abandon that birds, nesting in the surrounding trees, soared off into the night sky with matching screeches.

"Damn, what now?"

With adroitness born of terror, she managed to unzip her bag enough to release her arms. Joel, dear sweet Joel, was kneeling beside her. Would it matter if he were Jack the Ripper? Wrapping her arms tightly around his neck, she moaned. "Joel, oh, Joel, it's a snake."

"Cassie, for God's sake, let me go," he wheezed, "you're choking me."

Tightening her grip, she cried. "On my legs. On my legs."

Attempting to wrench her arms away, he staggered. She was drowning and he was a plank of wood. With heavy grunt, he managed to straighten, bringing Cassie, still cocooned in her sleeping bag, with him.

While not relinquishing her hold of his neck, she managed to kick her way out of the sleeping bag. With a flick of her legs, she straddled across his back, wrapping her legs securely around his waist. He gave a groan and fell to his hands and knees.

"Get off me, you're breaking my back."

Burying her face into his back, she cried. "Oh, no, no, no."

Stretching a hand behind him and grasping her around her waist, he dragged her until she swung beneath him clinging to him like a baby koala clung to its mother. Peering down at her through the darkness, he said in even tones, "Cassie, let me go."

"Never."

"Listen to me. If there is a snake, then we're going to be bitten to death unless you release me and I can investigate."

A tiny shred of sanity inched into her fear-stricken brain—her pounding-with-horror brain—her brain that would stop working unless somebody did something about getting rid of snakes. "Don't let me fall onto the ground."

Struggling to his feet, he juggled her onto his hip. "Where do you suggest I put you?"

"Preferably on asphalt."

He laughed, but he didn't put her down. Instead he stooped, and lifting her sleeping bag, gave it a hefty shake, placing it back onto the ground and lowered her on to it.

"If there'd been a snake," he assured her, "it would have well and truly gone by now. He's not going to stay around to be introduced. Trust me, he doesn't want trouble anymore than you do."

A flash of shadowy movement. "There, see, it's a opossum. He must have fallen out of the tree and landed on you."

Nestling close to him and wrapping one arm around his neck, she pressed her face against his bare chest. Her shoulders heaved. "Are you crying?"

She was laughing. "Oh, Joel, I lost it there for awhile." She laughed louder. He joined in. "A opossum. I was scared out of my brain over a opossum."

He chucked her under the chin. His eyes glinted in the blackness. "Do you want to sleep with Sam?"

"No. I'll get back in the sleeping bag. I'm not scared anymore."

He kissed the tip of her nose. "Cassie, Cassie. Do you know how much I want you?"

She sighed his name. "Joel." Her lips parted in sweet anticipation of his kiss. He pulled her into him, burying his face into her hair.

You smell like gum trees," he whispered. "Like a green field wet with spring rain."

Unable to resist him, she wound an arm around his neck and lowered his head to meet her eager lips. "Kiss me, Joel?"

"I thought you'd never ask," he said, and brushed his lips across hers. "I can't begin to tell you how much you mean to me—I want to tell you, Cassie, how—" He briefly closed his eyes and shook his head. "I'm tongue-tied. I feel like a school kid who's been found nicking sweets from a shop."

He drew her close to him and pressed his mouth against hers. The curve of her body molded against the strength of his. He tasted like eucalyptus, pine smoke, and wattle. He tasted good.

Fragrant perfumes assailed her mind.

This kiss would never end. She didn't want it to. She curled an arm around his neck, drawing him tighter into her embrace.

His hand touched her hair. "Your hair is as red as a summer sunset, wild as the storm. See how it slips through my fingers." His lips found the cradle of her neck. Her heart thundered in her ears as she heard him whisper, "Don't you understand? Don't you understand that I love you?"

And in that moment together in the sweet-smelling bushland her dreams, her hopes all came together with those three little words. *I love you.*

The truth, which had lain at the bottom of her heart for so long, stirred, and she thought the words she'd been so afraid of. *I love him.* She loved him and had done so since she'd first met him. He filled her heart. He was her life, her joy, her future, her everything.

Now she would never have to leave him. They would stay together on Oriole for the rest of their lives. She would ask for no more than this.

Joel had completed her life.

"Oh, Joel."

He drew back from her. "Do you know what I think?"

"What do you think?"

"I think you're in love with me."

She was enclosed by his love. "I am, I am."

"Marry me, Cassie. Be my wife. Stay with me on Oriole for the rest of our lives."

"Yes, yes, yes."

"How much do you love me? Tell me." His voice was thick with emotion. "Tell me."

"More than life itself."

"Through all eternity nothing can destroy our love." He kissed her gently at first and then with such force as if he couldn't get enough of her. Forever was the time their lips held. "Tell me," she murmured against his mouth. "How much do you love me?"

Pulling slightly back from her, she sensed that Joel outstretched his arms. "This much." He lowered his arm and clasped her hand. "Think there's enough room for me in your sleeping bag?"

She laughed gleefully. He slid one hand to her nape while the other tangled in the mass of her hair as he pulled her toward his mouth.

He loved her.

CHAPTER SIXTEEN

Cassie walked into the kitchen. "Hi, Berta. Got a coffee for a thirsty woman?"

"Nice and hot," Berta said pouring the coffee into a large mug and placing it before Cassie. "How'd the trip go? Did you have a great time?"

"Wonderful." Cassie swallowed down the desire to tell Berta that Joel had confessed his love for her. That everything between them was all right. That they would marry and she would stay with them on Oriole. They wanted to tell Queenie first. Her heart sang with delight.

"Sam's done nothing but talk, talk, talk about the trip and what he saw."

"It was such a wonderful experience for him." And for her.

"He loves Oriole."

"And everyone on it." And so did she.

"That's right, he does. The sweet little chap." Berta squeezed her arm. "And you're a wonderful girl."

Slightly surprised, Cassie answered, "Oh, I don't know about that."

"Yes, you are. Everything you're doing for Joel and the missus."

Confused, Cassie shook her head lightly. "Everything I'm doing? I don't understand."

Berta patted her hair. "That you've decided to leave Sam here. It's a great life for a little boy."

"Leave Sam here?" Cassie asked bewildered. "Whatever do you mean?"

The older woman measured some flour into a cup. "The missus told me about how Sam would be staying here permanently."

"That must have been when we came back from our trip." Maybe Berta had heard Joel telling his mother how he'd fallen in love with Cassie and planned to marry her. It surprised her that Joel had spoken to Queenie when they'd decided to tell her together.

Berta looked taken aback. "Oh no, it was before you came here. I was in her bedroom when Joel rang telling her how he'd found Sam. Tickled pink she was. The best I'd seen her for such a long time—all smiles and beams. 'He's bringing my grandson to Oriole,' she tells me. 'For a visit?' I ask. 'No,' she said, 'Joel will fix it so that Sam can stay here forever. Isn't it wonderful, Berta?'"

Please be wrong. "Is that exactly what she said, Berta? That Joel will fix it so that Sam can stay?"

This was exactly what Jane had told her to be aware of, and she'd gone blithely ahead ignoring the fact that Joel's main objective was to keep Sam on Oriole. She'd put her own hormonal desires at the forefront of her mind, clouded her common sense and her main objective in life—Sam.

Berta broke two eggs into a dish and whisked them. "Yes, those are the words. I remember how excited we were that a child would be growing up here on Oriole. Anyhow, I've been meaning to tell you for a long while how lovely it is that you'll be leaving Sam here with us. He'll be better off here than in the smoggy city. And the missus will—"

Cassie legs nearly gave way beneath her as she staggered towards the door.

"Where are you going?" Berta called. "I'm making some pancakes."

"I've forgotten something in my room," Cassie managed to say. "I'll be back in a moment."

She walked out of the kitchen, stumbled to the front door, and almost fell out onto the veranda.

He wanted to keep Sam and he'd pay any cost. He'd played her for a fool. Planned for her to fall in love with him probably from the moment he'd met her. How easy she had made it for him. One word of love and she'd fallen into his arms like the lovesick fool she was. A pat on his back. Congratulations all round on winning his prize so easily.

Joel had lied when he'd said he loved her, and marrying her made it easy for him to have what he desired—Sam permanently on Oriole. The acid rose from the pit of her stomach to the back of her throat. And her heart beat scarily in her ears.

Tears threatened.

She leaned against a railing and wrapped her arms around her chest.

He'd twisted her around until she had believed he'd loved her, and it wasn't true—he wanted only Sam. She had known this from the very beginning and she'd chosen to ignore it because she wanted to sleep with him!

Among the sorrow came a deep sense of shame and humiliation that she had so willingly confessed her love for him. He didn't love her, and he would never love her. And that was something she would have to accept and deal with.

If Berta in all her innocence hadn't told her the truth, Cassie would never have known any difference.

Suddenly cold, she wrapped her arms around her breasts, rubbing her arms. She wished that Berta had never told her of the conversation she had had with Queenie. Had Cassie not learned the truth maybe Joel would, in the fullness of time, have learned to love her. Then she could have stayed with him here on Oriole; Sam would grow big and strong like his uncle. But that wouldn't have happened. If he didn't love her now, he'd never love her. Their life together would have been built on a lie and like a house of cards would have tumbled around them before very long.

Tears burned, and she rubbed the back of her hand across her eyes. Now for the first time in a long time, she wanted to wallow in self-pity. So what. Was that a crime? Couldn't she do that and not feel so damn guilty? Why shouldn't she feel bad and miserable when she couldn't have the one thing she wanted most in life?

Joel, oh, Joel.

And she was angry. Angry for becoming sentimental, overly romantic, and weak enough to love Joel when her heart should have remained steel-encased from him.

If only Joel had been content to share him. If only he hadn't wanted to keep Sam on Oriole through lies and deceit.

Cassie's thoughts blew through her head like tumbleweeds.

He doesn't love me.

He only wants Sam.

I love him so damn much it hurts.

With a sense of deep sadness, she knew she would leave him. Return to Melbourne and try to get her life back together, but somehow she doubted that she could—that it would be impossible for her to function normally again.

So what would become of her?

She didn't know, she just didn't know.

She wanted…she wanted …

A sob escaped her lips and her throat closed over as scalding tears finally released and slid down her cheeks. It didn't matter what she wanted. She would never believe that he truly loved her. Whatever could he do or say to convince her of his love when she faced him with the truth of what she had learned?

Hopeless. It was all so hopeless.

Despair blazed into anger and she clenched her hands into fists. She would accuse Joel with her newly found knowledge. Tell him how much she despised him for being cruel and insensitive, and he would have to admit the truth. Then it would be easy for her to leave him.

And once she left, she would never return.

CHAPTER SEVENTEEN

Joel had never known such happiness. They would marry as quickly as possible. Then their wonderful life would begin here on Oriole. There wasn't anything he wouldn't do for Cassie. He would bathe her in diamonds. Take her to exotic places she'd only read about. His love for her was absolute, as strong and indestructible as the mountains.

He remembered the perfume of her hair. The sweetness of her lips. The fire of her embrace.

He'd had a busy day on the station with a breach birth foal and one of the men quitting without warning. It'd taken Joel a long time to talk the man around and convince him to stay, at least until Joel could find a replacement. By the time he'd come back to the house everyone had retired for the night. He'd hesitated outside Cassie's bedroom, desperate to talk to her, see her. *Take it easy, plenty of time.* They had the rest of their lives together.

He rose from his bed and walked to the window. He stared out upon Oriole.

The station was a different place at night. So quiet and peaceful you could hear the softest rustle of a opossum or the hoot of an owl. He glanced at the sky. The moon sat fat and yellow, queen of all she surveyed. Its muted streams of light cascaded through the trees and spotlighted the earth in pools of creamy luster.

A zillion diamonds had been scooped from the bowels of the earth and flung up into the midnight blackness of the sky. They glittered and glistened for all to see but none to own.

Happiness, strong and total, descended on him.

CHAPTER EIGHTEEN

Joel couldn't sleep. He made his way quietly down the stairs, hesitating at the bottom, unsure what he wanted to do or where he wanted to go.

He swerved in his direction and headed toward the indoor pool at the back of the house. He groped for the key, which was kept on the ledge above the door. The door to the pool had been securely locked since Sam had made his presence known at Oriole. Unlocking the door, he returned the key to its resting place and locked the door behind him.

He approached the edge of the pool and stared into its blue crystal depths. His shadowy reflection shimmered back at him. Stripping naked, he dived deep. He spun over on to his stomach and through the moon's soft glow, there was Cassie.

She removed her terry towel wraparound, adjusted the straps of her swimsuit, and plunged deep into the pool. His limbs, much more powerful than hers, shortened the distance between them swiftly.

He heard her gasp as his hands spanned her waist.

"Joel, you scared me half to death."

Their bodies entwined. He drew her down into the depths of the pool. She wrapped her arms around his neck and a feeling of total love overtook him. His lips moved over hers and they kissed, hungrily, hotly.

They broke the surface, gasping for air. Again, he claimed her mouth.

Their mouths clung as he drifted them to the edge of the pool. He hoisted himself out and lowered his hands. Trustingly, willingly, she placed her hands in his, and he scooped her out and into his arms.

Gently, he lowered her to the floor. He lay slightly away from her, lifting the wet hair that clung to her face and neck. "Have I told you that you drive me crazy?" he told her softly.

"Joel, Joel," she murmured reaching up to touch the wetness of his hair. Her warm breath whispered across his brow and then, to his utter dismay, she cried.

Pain seized his heart as he grabbed her to him. "Love, don't cry," he begged. "Tell me what's wrong and I'll make it right."

He couldn't help but kiss her. Her mouth warm and soft beneath his. A gentle kiss. A kiss of love and not passion. It was a foretelling kiss. In this kiss he put all his emotion, all the feelings he carried for her. He knew no other way to tell her.

It was forever before he yielded her mouth.

"You taste like strawberries," he whispered, and he trailed his lips down the side of her neck to gently probe the hollows at the base of her throat. "I love you. Love you." His desire for her grew. He wanted to make love her with her here, now. His need for her was paramount.

She drew away from him. "I don't believe you, Joel," she said sadly.

It would have hurt less if she had slapped him across his face. Desire dissolved and in its stead confusion mingled with fear. "Not believe me?" he said hesitantly. "I don't understand."

She sat up, and drawing up her knees, wrapped her arms around them. "Berta told me you planned on keeping Sam from the very beginning. She was in Queenie's bedroom when you told her."

He sat erect. "What?"

Her face flushed as she brushed the wet strands of her hair from her face. "Don't deny it. For God's sake, tell the truth."

Death crossed the threshold to his heart. "Idle words, that's all."

She wiped her eyes with the back of her hand. "Idle, nothing. You meant to keep Sam at all cost. I'm shattered by your lies. I believed it was me you wanted and were in love with." She drew in a deep, stabilizing breath.

Words eluded him as he listened, dumbstruck.

"You'd do anything, Joel? Even make love to me perhaps? Marry me? My God, what a sacrifice." She gave a sob. "Would you go to those lengths? Is that how low you would stoop to get what you want?"

His life crashed around him and his dream of marrying Cassie and living together on Oriole dissolved under her undeniable accusation. What could he do? What could he say to make her believe that he loved her? Whatever he said would surely sound ineffectual and untrue. God, what an unholy mess.

"Sometimes things aren't what they seem, and it's difficult to explain, to make it right." He glanced at her pale face.

Her eyes wide and anxious, she said, "Did you intend to keep Sam on Oriole at any price?"

He wanted to deny and say that he'd never spoken those words to Queenie. "Whatever I say won't sound right."

"Tell me, Joel. Answer me."

"Yes."

Her body slumped. "I knew it. All the time I knew it, yet I hoped and prayed it wouldn't be true."

"That was before I knew I loved you," he cried, wanting her to know, wanting her to understand. How could he make her understand that at the beginning that was all he wanted—to keep Sam with him? He never anticipated falling in love with Cassie. That was something that just happened. Was he now going to lose her?

He briefly closed his eyes. Not again. Not again. He couldn't take this a second time. To love and have that love ripped out of his heart as if a savage beast had clawed its way inside his chest.

"You lied to me just to get what you wanted," he heard her say. Her eyes were so sad, almost as sad as his heart. "You were willing to marry me to keep Sam." Through the moonlight her tears glistened. He wanted to comfort her. He had no idea how.

"Your vows of love. Your promises, all shadows on the wall. Joel, Joel, you've drained my heart. Have you any idea how I feel?"

I'm going to lose her. Sweet Christ, don't let me lose her.

The guilt of his selfishness, the consequences of his actions were coming back to bite. He knew of no way to make things right for them. A flash of loneliness stabbed him. "I would never hurt you or Sam," he managed at last. "I told you from the beginning that I wanted to take you into consideration with regards to Sam, and we agreed that something could be worked out.

"Somewhere along the way, I fell in love with you, and I thought everything would be okay. That we would marry and you'd live here with me. I never lied when I said I loved you. Cassie, you must believe me. I love you with all my heart."

"Believe you love me? How can I ever do that?" Her gaze was cold as it connected with his.

He straightened his shoulders, drew in a long steadying breath. "Then take Sam and leave Oriole."

• • •

"What?"

"I said take Sam and go. Leave Oriole tomorrow. I'll make all the necessary arrangements." His expression was that of a man who had been struck in the face. "I'll never bother either of you again. You'll never hear from me again," he said wretchedly. "You can pretend I never happened. That we never happened."

"You want us to leave Oriole—leave you?" She struggled with the words because her mind was fogged over with confusion.

He walked to the edge of the pool and struggled into his jeans. He turned and connected with her gaze. "It's all I know to do."

"But you love Sam so very much."

His eyes were so sad, so empty and alone, her heart lurched and the pain was terrible. "I love you more," he said simply.

"Joel," she whispered. "Oh, Joel." She moved to stand in front of him and, reaching over, stroked his face with her fingertips.

He placed his hands on her cheeks and kissed her on the forehead. "I wanted Sam in the beginning, and I would have done anything to keep him here on Oriole, and then I realized how cruel it would be to take Sam away from the only mother he's ever known. I couldn't do that to you or him. I love you both so much."

He reached out and touched her hair with his big hand. Her heartbeat was joyous. Happiness descended as her life with Joel and Sam on Oriole stretched out before her.

"I love you. With all my heart, with all my soul. Do you forgive me, Cassie? Can you give me a second chance?"

He held open his arms and she fell into them. "Joel, Joel," she cried.

Reaching up and curling her arms around his neck, she forced his head down so she could kiss his lips. She never wanted to stop kissing him.

He crushed her to him and smothered her face with his kisses. Her forehead, her eyes, her cheeks and at last her eager mouth. "My love." He took her by the hand. "Come with me."

She followed him upstairs and into his bedroom. He went to a tall dresser and took out a small box, which he handed to her. "This is for you," he said.

"What is it?"

He smiled. "Open it."

She did as he bid and withdrew a dainty silver bracelet from which hung an American Civil War dime. "The dime your father gave your mother."

"No. This is a dime I give to you. It's my way of telling you how much I love you, Cassie. That you are the only woman for me now and forever. That I love you beyond life itself."

"Oh, Joel."

"I loved you before we went on our camping trip, so I set the wheels in motion to find a dime. I wanted to give you something to show my love for you. I thought about the dime my father gave to my mother and with a great deal of effort, I found this one and had it made into a bracelet for you." He touched her hair. "It was to be your wedding gift."

"Joel."

He drew her into the safety of his arms. "I love you so much it hurts my heart."

She snuggled into his chest. "This is the beginning of the rest of our lives."

"Only the beginning."

With joyous laughter they fell upon the bed and became consumed with each other.

Knowing this was how it would be for the rest of their lives.

CHAPTER NINETEEN

Cassie withheld from wearing the time-honored bridal gear. Instead she chose to wear a soft, floaty cream silken slip that skimmed her body, covered by a light-as-air taupe coat. Tiny frangipanis adorned her hair in a halo of ivory perfume; beige-colored satin sandals and a tiny bouquet of creamy roses and baby's breath completed the perfect picture.

As Cassie walked down the stairs with Sam by her side, her heart was bursting from happiness. Who would have thought today would have ever come? That she was to marry Joel? It was all too wonderful to be true.

Sam tugged her dress, and she stopped and knelt down in front of him. "We're marrying my Uncle Joel today, aren't we, Aunty C?"

"Yes, darling," she said automatically straightening the collar of his white shirt, correcting the tilt of his tiny, pink bow tie. He looked so cute in his cotton suit of pale blue.

"And then we never have to leave Oriole or Uncle Joel or Bluey or—"

"Sam, Sam." She laughed. "You'll never have to leave anyone you love ever."

"And when you marry my Uncle Joel you can go to the hospital, and get brothers and sisters for me to play with. Won't you, Aunty C?"

"Oh, love, I hope so. I truly hope so."

Standing, she took Sam's hand, and walked downstairs and out on to the veranda.

And then they were walking towards Joel. He turned and his face lit up with the profound love he had for them. And her heart beat strongly with pride and love.

Reaching down, Joel swept Sam up into his arms. "Ready to get us married, Tiger?" The child nodded eagerly.

Holding Sam with one arm, his other encased around Cassie's waist, they turned towards the celebrant.

"We are gathered here today to celebrate one of life's greatest moments," the celebrant began, "to give recognition to the worth and beauty of love, and to add our best wishes to the words that shall unite Cassandra and Joel in marriage.

"Cassie and Joel have asked me to read what Paul wrote of love in a letter to the Corinthians.

"Love is very patient and kind, never jealous or envious, never boastful or proud. Love is never haughty or selfish or rude. Love does not demand its own way. Love is not irritable or touchy. Love does not hold grudges and will hardly notice when others do it wrong. Love is never glad about injustice but rejoices whenever truth wins out. If you love someone, you will be loyal to them no matter what the costs. You will always believe in them, always expect the best in them, and will always stand your ground in defending them.

"The rings?" the celebrant asked, and Bluey, standing in as best man, placed the gold bands on the open page of the Bible the celebrant held while Cassie handed Jane her bouquet. Jane sent Cassie a wink and with a grin, she winked back.

"Wedding rings are an outward and visible sign of an inward spiritual grace, and the unbroken circle of love, signifying to all the union of this man and this woman in marriage. Joel and Cassandra, I now declare you to be husband and wife. Congratulations, you may kiss the bride."

Joel bent his head and crushed her mouth beneath his. She entwined her arms around her husband and Sam, locking them into her embrace, close to her heart, the two people she loved most in life.

• • •

Inside the Beechcraft, Joel turned to Cassie and said, "Ready for our honeymoon, darling?"

She touched his cheek with her fingertips. "Yes, my love."

And a tiny voice from the back of the plane chorused, "Me too, Uncle."

Berta's Famous Lamington Recipe

Ingredients

125 grams butter, softened
1 cup caster sugar
½ teaspoon vanilla extract
3 eggs
1¾ cups self-raising flour, sifted
½ cup milk
2 cups desiccated coconut

Icing

3½ cups icing sugar mixture
¼ cup cocoa powder
1 tablespoon butter, softened
½ cup boiling water

Method

1. Preheat oven to 180°C/160°C fan-forced (350°F). Grease a 20 cm × 30 cm (8" × 11") pan. Line with baking paper, leaving a 2 cm (¾") overhang on all sides. Using an electric mixer, beat butter, sugar and vanilla until light and fluffy. Add eggs, 1 at a time, beating well after each addition (mixture may curdle).

2. Sift half the flour over butter mixture. Stir to combine. Add half the milk. Stir to combine. Repeat with remaining flour and milk. Spoon into prepared pan. Smooth top. Bake for 30 minutes or until a skewer inserted in centre comes out clean. Leave in pan for 10 minutes. Turn out onto a wire rack. Cover with a clean kitchen cloth. Set aside overnight.

3. Make icing: Sift icing sugar and cocoa into a bowl. Add butter and boiling water. Stir until smooth.

4. Cut cake into 15 pieces. Place coconut in a dish. Using a fork, dip 1 piece of cake in icing. Shake off excess. Toss in coconut. Place on a wire rack. Repeat with remaining cake, icing and coconut. Stand for 2 hours or until set. Serve.

More from Crimson Romance
(From *A Taste of Honey*)

Courtship is a lost art.

"Are you okay, Charli? It's a shock, but I didn't know how else to tell you."

Judy Jenkins' voice bit into the sad confusion of her mind. "When did it happen?"

"Last night."

She clenched her bottom lip. This was so sad. Grief tore at Charli's heart. "Poor Mr. Knight. How did he—did he suffer?"

"His ticker gave out. He died in his sleep. He didn't feel a thing, Charli. Just didn't wake up, that's all." Judy came around her desk and gave her a warm hug. "Are you okay? You're such a softie."

She nodded. A thick knot caught somewhere in Charli's throat. She couldn't swallow. She was going to cry. She just knew she was. It was the shock. One moment she was joking and talking to Mr. Knight and the next he was gone. It was such an unreal sensation.

She looked over at his office door as if expecting him to poke around his head and say, "Any coffee, Charli?" Knowing full well she always had coffee percolating and iced buns in the stationery cupboard, a particular favorite of his.

"Was he alone?"

Judy gave a wry smile. "Only you'd ask that question, Charli. He was in bed and since I don't think Mr. Knight had any love interest since his wife died, he was alone."

She pulled herself erect. "Judy, you know what I meant. Was he alone in the house?"

"Yes, he was alone. His housekeeper found him this morning."

She'd been so fond of Mr. Knight, and now she'd never see him again. It was too awful to bear. "He said he didn't feel well. He complained of pain in the chest. I told him to go home and rest, but he wouldn't. He said he'd be all right." She ran her fingertips lightly across her brow. "I should have insisted."

"Now don't go and blame yourself. You couldn't have known how ill he really was. Anyway he was bull-headed and always did exactly what he wanted."

Tears dripped down her face. "He was a very private person." She groped into her desk drawer for a box of tissues. Plucking one, she blew her nose loudly. "He always had time to listen to my woes."

"He took a special interest in you; protective, like a dad would be, and he wouldn't have a word said against you, no way."

Charli smiled at the memory. Mr. Knight was considerate toward her. His greatest desire was to see her married to a nice man who'd look after her. He believed in the sanctity of marriage. The blessed union of one man and one woman until *death do us part.*

Get married, Charli, he'd said. It's the only way to a contented life. And she'd smile and say she hadn't met Mr. Right.

She was old-fashioned in her outlook on romance. She wanted to be courted like her father had courted her mother. She'd loved hearing the tales her mother told her about how her father had taken her out to dinner, bringing her chocolate and flowers. They picnicked at the beach and danced to a blues jazz band at the local dancehall. He wooed her until she fell in love with him, and he'd finally proposed and she'd gladly accepted. So romantic.

She didn't expect a knight in shining armor on a white steed sort of thing, but a man who knew how to court a woman. How to make her feel special, assuring her that he'd do anything for her that was within his power.

"His work was his life." Her eyes flew to Judy's. "His work? What will become of the business now?"

"There's a nephew, William Knight. I've heard he's coming to take over the reins."

"Does he know anything about publishing?"

"He runs a small publishing house in Darwin."

Surprised, she said, "I didn't know anything about that. Mr. Knight didn't mention he even had a nephew."

Judy was the office receptionist, and besides the fact that she'd been working here for years, what she didn't know about everyone in the office wasn't worth knowing. Mr. Knight always said that Judy had radar implanted in her brain. It focused in on all the office gossip. It wasn't that Judy was malicious; to the contrary, she had a warm and giving heart. She was a natural born sticky-beak and loved to know everybody's business.

"Don't suppose he wanted to talk about it. The family was in shock for years."

"Shock? What were they shocked about?"

"Over what happened to his nephew."

Had William Knight taken a car on a joy ride in his youth? Or maybe tax evasion or failing to stop at a red light. "Something bad happened to his nephew?"

"Too bloody right it did."

Her interest piqued. Charli leant forward and said, "Don't leave out a thing, Judy. Tell me all."

"Young Mr. Knight fell in love with his chief editor. They married, and a few years later, she ran off with his star author, taking half of his most popular writers with her. She started up her own business here in Melbourne. Might have heard of it. Powerful Press."

"Yes, I have." Charli loved gossip. What woman didn't? "Tell me more."

"Nothing more to tell. Young Mr. Knight struggled to keep his business afloat, and through hard decision-making and sheer business brilliance managed to do so."

"This is so unbelievably juicy," she said.

"He should have sued the pants off her."

"Don't be so pedantic, Judy. She was a witch with a capital B." Charli placed a hand over her heart and said, "She broke his heart. Our Young Mr. Knight is sensitive and obviously very romantic."

Would William Knight be a younger version of his uncle, short, slightly overweight, balding? Well, perhaps not balding, but hair receding slightly at the temples and forehead; a friendly man with a boisterous laugh and generous disposition who would visit the office twice, three times a week, just to keep his finger in the pie.

A beautiful vision came into her mind. *"Miss Honey, I need to express myself with my art and wish to lock myself in a turret and paint. So therefore I'm giving you a promotion and putting you in charge of running Knight Books. You are more than capable."*

A surge of excitement. This was her big opportunity, she just knew it.

"Ah, well, not my business." Judy contradicted and Charli hid a smile. "Wanna do lunch?"

"That'd be great."

"See you at one."

Charli walked to her office window; the day was wet and windy as only Melbourne could be in May. She gazed out on to the multistory buildings. Everything must be perfect for the new boss. She would impress him with her professionalism; her efficiency; and, if he chose to stay at the helm, become his reliable right-hand.

In her mind's eye she saw herself standing side-by-side with young Mr. Knight. They were staring off into the not-too-distant future. The wind was blowing through her hair, a look of grim determination on her face and his arm draped around her shoulders. No, no, too intimate. Shoulder to shoulder. Sort of like Leonardo DiCaprio and Kate Winslet in Titanic standing at the helm, or was it starboard? Their love much stronger than their fear of death. So romantic, she'd seen the movie four times.

Sighing deeply, she returned to her desk and made notes on a pad. Leaning back in her chair, she tapped her lower teeth with the end of a pen. Number one, she had to sort through Mr. Knight's papers, and he wasn't the tidiest of men, bluntly refusing to let her organize his desk when her hands were itching to do so.

There was a lot to do before his nephew arrived.

Would he, as she hoped, pass the running of Knight Books on to her, or would he have completely different ideas from his uncle on how to run the company? Either way, she could cope. She was a professional and knew the ropes. He would have to read her work reports and know how proficient she was and how she was an asset to Knight Books.

She threw the pen onto her desk. "Time will tell," she said aloud. "Time will tell."

• • •

William Knight sighed. He hadn't quite come to terms with the loss of his uncle. Now it was only his mother and him. It hadn't been easy, but he'd come to a decision. Leave Darwin in the capable hands of Stan McFee and take up the reins of Knight Books. He could think of no alternative.

Going back to Melbourne struck his quivering nerves like a snapped guitar string. He pushed his thumbs into the pits of his eyes and cursed softly. Darwin not being big enough for the two of them, Mavis's words not his, she'd scurried off to Melbourne with Brad Wilde, his top writer, clinging to her side. She'd betrayed him both personally and professionally.

He'd fallen for Mavis's dark beauty hook, line, and sinker. Taught her the ropes of running a publishing house, and, without warning, she'd started her own business and taken every worthwhile author she could with her. Charmed and armed, that was Mavis. Planned every move she'd ever made.

There'd be no escaping running into her at some time or another in Melbourne. How would he handle that ugly situation? Smile and a handshake, or snarl and turn his back?

Her stabbing him in the back didn't happen immediately. It took years of clever planning, learning the ropes, ingratiating herself with everybody. Hell, even the cleaner loved Mavis and lit up like a Christmas tree every time she spoke to him. Come to think of it, he went with her too.

If she never gave him anything else, she'd given him a deep mistrust of women in business. He'd never work hand-in-glove with a woman again. He didn't trust their soft smiles. The enticing lure that lay deep in their baby blues like a dangling worm to an unsuspecting fish. He'd learned a hard lesson and he'd learned it well.

He looked up as Stan McFee ambled into his office. He liked Stan very much and they'd become firm friends over the years. Often he had dinner with Stan and his wife, Lauren, a beautiful ex-model that men gave prolonged lustful looks. Will knew her as a woman whose life revolved around her family's happiness. When they'd made Lauren, they had thrown away the mold. "All set to go, Will?"

"Yeah. Ready but not quite willing. Think you can handle things here, Stan?"

"You've asked me that question a hundred times."

"Sorry."

"That's okay." He flung his long frame into a chair, stretching out his legs in front of him. "So you know who you'll be working with?"

"Charles Honey. And by all accounts, he's one capable chief editor." He glanced at Honey's work reports. "Funny thing, Stan.

He's only temporary in the position. My uncle never made him permanent chief editor. No worries. I'll tidy that up quick smart."

"So all your worries were for nothing?"

"It's made me feel easier having a man working with me. I couldn't take a woman, Stan. No way. I'd go nuts."

Stan laughed. "Your reputation laughs at your denial, Will. You're a woman's man from way back."

"I'm not talking about my private life. You know what I mean."

"Not every woman in business is like your ex."

"I have no qualms about women in business, what I don't want is a woman working side by side with me. Now I won't have to face that. Thank God for Charles Honey."

Will pushed himself back in his chair. It wouldn't be so bad. Running Knight Books was the challenge he needed. He was getting soft here in Darwin. Back in the big time was called for. Charles Honey was a top man. Yeah, things were going to be okay.

• • •

Charli had hoped she'd meet young Mr. Knight at the funeral. As it turned out it was only a small service in the chapel with sandwiches and coffee later. She'd asked around but it had appeared that young Mr. Knight had left immediately after the service. She consoled herself she'd meet him soon enough.

No sooner than she'd thought that, a fax arrived stating that William Knight would be arriving at the office early the next day.

Charli had Malcolm Knight's office thoroughly cleaned in preparation for William Knight's arrival. She moved into his office and glanced around. Maybe she should get some flowers as a welcome from the staff. She buzzed the intercom. "Yes, Charli?"

"Judy, order some long-stemmed yellow roses and irises to be delivered first thing in the morning—no, have them delivered now. You never know, our young Mr. Knight may get here sooner than he said."

"Sure thing, Charli."

"And, Judy."

"Yes?"

"Don't stint on them. We want Mr. Knight to feel very welcome for his first day with us."

She studied the desk once more, everything in its place and a place for everything. She moved the telephone a fraction toward the edge of the desk, bringing his desk lamp a little further toward his chair.

Hands on her hips, she said aloud, "I think our young Mr. Knight should be content with his office. I can't wait to meet you, William Knight. If you're half as nice as your uncle then we should have a good working relationship."

In the mood for more Crimson Romance?
Check out *Enlisted by Love*
by Jenny Jacobs
at *CrimsonRomance.com.*

www.ingramcontent.com/pod-product-compliance
Lightning Source LLC
Chambersburg PA
CBHW010640100726
47900CB00011B/2908